Glit-er-ary

Glit-er-ary

an anthology

Edited by Debz Hobbs-Wyatt and Gill James

Bridge House

British Library Cataloguing in Publication Data

A Record of this Publication is available from the British Library

ISBN 978-1-907335-55-6

This edition published 2017 by Bridge House Publishing
Manchester, England

All Bridge House books are published on paper derived from sustainable resources.

Contents

Introduction

I have had the great pleasure of working for Bridge House now for some years. When it all started I was just a writer with a dream. It was the fabulous Gill James, and her notion of becoming a publisher, that lead us here, many books later. Gill gave me my first publishing credit in Bridge House's first anthology, *Making Changes*, back in 2008. Next year we celebrate ten years of publishing short stories! After that first story I had a few successes with Bridge House before I joined her and took on a role in marketing, and later as an editor and working alongside Gill.

This year, our little company has expanded again, now set to publish single-author collections, a commisioned collection that I was asked to contribute to and a few other well-known writers... so there's plenty still to come!

At one time our love and passion for books and the short story form (probably added to by a nice evening with free-flowing wine) lead us to publish some eight themed collections in one year. Even we knew that was a little overzealous. But hey... After that we took it back to one collection of the best, and all kinds of unusual slightly less obvious themes. But they all have one thing in common: we love stories that make us think, that stretch our imagination, that are a little different. Though the stories are not Christmas tales per se, they do come out in the festive season and follow the form we used in *Making Changes*, an idea that we have twenty-four stories, one for every day of Advent. It's like opening a door and wondering what treat is inside. And so, with that in mind, we've had collections called *Snowflakes*, *Baubles* and this year *Glit-er-rary*.

At the annual launch event last year, Gill suddenly asked me, "So Debz, what is the theme for next year?" And I said the first word that came into my head: Gliterary! I had been asked last year to take part in the annual Christmas Tree Festival where my writing group meets, and we decided to have a writing-themed tree that we called The Gliterary Tree. With that still fresh in my mind, it seemed a great name for a collection of tales with a literary edge and a touch of sparkle

So that is what you have here. Our wonderful writers once again embraced the theme, and what you see here are the ones that stood out from all the submissions we received. So please do welcome new writers alongside more established ones in this wonderful collection.

Why do we keep doing it? Simple: for love and for our passion. Do any of us make money? Well no, we give a lot to charity through some of our collections, but the rest gets invested in the next book. But one thing I know for sure is that no matter what, Gill and I will continue to wave that banner for the short story form, give writers somewhere to see their work in print, and provide a place for readers to hang out and enjoy the plethora of talent waiting to be discovered.

Debz Hobbs-Wyatt

A Little Bit of Sparkle

Elizabeth Cox

Ruth pulled her summer jacket tightly around her and zipped it up. Even though it was still August, it had been raining earlier and the sky was overcast. She hurried to the pay station to get a ticket for her car, as she was running late. Her friends would think she had stood them up. Hunger was eating away at her; she was eager for her coffee and scone. Without looking where she was going, she was scrabbling in her bag to find loose pound coins in the voluminous interior, when she stumbled. As she steadied herself on the wet metal pole, there on the floor she saw a pair of child's trainers, silver and covered with sequins. Neatly placed side by side, as if left there on purpose. They were filled with rain water.

She looked around her, thinking that someone had just put them down while on a similar mission to herself and had simply forgotten to pick them up. But there was no one to be seen. She reasoned that they must have been left there some time ago to be so full of dirty water. She didn't know what to do. Should she tip the water out? She might save the shoes from becoming soaked through, but looking at them it appeared to be too late for that. Should she pick them up? No, someone might remember where they left them and come looking. It would be unfair for her to take them away. No, she would leave them. She expected they would have been retrieved by the time she left the café.

As Ruth crossed the road to meet her friends her thoughts were occupied by the shoes to such an extent that she almost walked under a black car, only brought out of her daydream by the angry honking of a car horn. Smiling a vague apology, she raised her hand to the irate driver and continued towards the café.

She met her friends here each week for coffee and a chat. It got her out of the house, but she never felt completely at home there. As she pushed on the chrome handle of the smoked glass door, it opened silently in her path. The clacking of her heels across the grey tiled floor of the entrance, caused all eyes to be raised and glance in her direction. The room was full this afternoon and smelled of wet coats and coffee. Black and chrome chairs were scraped across the light beech floor of the dining area, as people turned back to their conversations. As she moved across the floor, she pretended to look at the abstract art from local artists which adorned the grey walls; the only bright spot in a dreary room. Her friends were waiting, coffee cooling, as she approached.

"Hello everyone, I'm sorry I'm late, I was distracted by the strangest thing." The waiting women looked at each other and raised their eyebrows.

"Go on, do tell," her best friend Janet encouraged, as she summoned the waitress with an imperious wave of her bony hand. A young girl with a row of piercings along her ear lobe sauntered over, shuffling her feet across the scuffed floor.

"Yes," she sniffed.

"Four coffees please and take these dirty cups away." The girl turned away, leaving the cups behind.

Ruth smiled apologetically at the tattooed girl, "Leave her alone, Janet, she's only a child."

"Tell me what distracted you." Janet's acerbic voice brought Ruth back to reality.

"Well," said Ruth not knowing where to start. "When I was leaving the carpark, at the bottom pay station, there was a pair of child's silver trainers, covered in pretty sequins."

"What's so special about that?" Janet's interest had waned, as she was expecting something more salacious.

"They were placed neatly, side by side, which seemed oddly deliberate to me. And they were filled with rain water."

"Some careless child left them there I expect. Nothing unusual about that. Careless little blighters, children." Janet, who didn't suffer fools gladly, was bored with the subject now and was stacking the dirty cups, as the waitress reappeared with the coffees, slopping the contents into their saucers. Ruth looked as if she had been slapped across the face, but smoothed her skirt down and said nothing. The others glanced at each other. Janet could be so insensitive sometimes.

The subject of the shoes was soon forgotten in the general conversation that followed, but not by Ruth. Round and round in her mind a picture of the shoes turned like a kaleidoscope, sequins flashing blue and red and purple.

"I've got to go," Ruth pushed her chair back with a scrape, grabbed her paisley scarf and large leather handbag and fled. Her friends stared in amazement.

"What's wrong with Ruth this afternoon?" Pauline drawled, flicking back her blonde fringe. "She's not a creature of impulse normally."

"She did seem a bit odd, something to do with those shoes I expect," said Annabel, a petite brunette wearing a thick sweater and old jeans. "You can never tell with Ruth."

The others looked to Janet for her opinion on this unusual situation.

"Who knows," shrugged Janet, sipping her coffee and negotiating a cream slice.

Ruth ran to the carpark. What if the shoes were no longer there? What would she do if they had gone? As she reached the pay station, she could see the shoes gleaming in the sun, the sequins turning orange and red now. They were still sitting side by side on the tarmac. No one had come for them. They were hers. She skipped the last few steps across the road, despite her aching hip. Picking up the shoes, she carefully tipped the water out onto the floor and caressed the shoes dry with her paisley scarf, the one Alan had bought her for her last birthday. There, they were lovely and dry now, look at how the sequins were shining. She flicked a damp leaf from the toe of the right shoe, buffed them once again with her scarf and placed them neatly together in her bag. She patted the bag and turned towards her car. Tilly would love them.

She laid the bag carefully on the passenger seat, so as not to upset the shoes onto the floor of the car which was rather grubby, and draped her scarf carefully over the bag to shield its contents. All the way home she sang along with the car radio; Eddie Cochran, Cliff Richard, Ed Sheeran, Rod Stewart, Katy Perry, tapping her chewed finger nails on the steering wheel in time to the music. This was a good day.

When she arrived home, Alan was already there. His golf match must have finished early, and he was in the kitchen putting the kettle on. She had to tell him.

"Guess what I've got for Tilly?" she blurted out unable to contain her excitement.

"Now, love," said Alan, "come and have a nice cup of tea. It's ready and I've put some chocolate digestives out as well." He placed the mugs on the pine table, then turned to get the teapot.

"Alan, you have to see, they're so lovely, Tilly will be thrilled."

Alan sighed and turned to look at her, the plate of biscuits still in his hand.

"What have you brought?" Alan was tall and spare with

thick grey hair which he wore closely cropped. His face was tanned yet etched with lines.

"Look here they are," Ruth exclaimed, unwrapping the shoes from her scarf with a flourish. She placed them neatly side by side on the table, then ran her fingers through her curly red hair, streaked with grey at the temples. "This is how I found them, but they're a bit wet inside. They were filled with rainwater. I'll have to dry them out properly, before I give them to Tilly." The shoes twinkled at her, as if delighted to be in her company.

"But Tilly can't wear them my love, you know that." Alan spoke patiently but Ruth, distraught, grabbed the shoes from the table and turned for the stairs.

"You don't understand. Yes she can, of course she can! She'll love them." Ruth ran up the stairs clutching the sequinned trainers in her hand, her hoarse voice trailing in her wake. She tripped up the last step and reached for the second door on the landing grabbing the handle. A plaque on the door said "Tilly's Room" picked out in gold letters on the cream painted wood. She turned the handle and entered the room. Illuminated by fairy lights which she kept on all the time, the room glowed with pink; flowery curtains and pale pink walls contributed to the womb like feeling of the space. She smiled and closed the door quietly behind her, inhaling the scent of the roses that she always kept there. Her soft whisper filled the empty space.

"Here you are, Tilly, just for you, I know you'll love them."

Ruth closed her eyes, imagining Tilly slipping her feet into the glittering shoes. She watched her tie the silver laces in a big bow, then grin up at her mother, her childish eyes, shining, as she twirled her feet around under the fairy lights to make the sequins gleam. Happiness engulfed her.

Alan followed Ruth up the stairs wearily, his hand

13

gripping the pine bannister, his knuckles white. He turned the door handle, entering the room behind her just as she was placing the shoes side by side on the narrow bed, smoothing the flowery bedspread, as she did so. His face crumpled with sadness. Turning to Alan, Ruth whispered, her face alight,

"There, when she comes home from school, they'll be ready for her."

"But Ruth," said Alan, taking hold of his wife tightly, "you know she won't be coming home from school." For an instant Ruth was defiant, but then her shoulders slumped. Her knees buckled, as he held her. She laid her head on his shoulder, her eyes glittering, reflecting the sequins on the lost shoes.

Elizabeth Cox

Born in Yorkshire and now residing in Anglesey, Elizabeth spends her time working at the 'day job' and writing short stories, poetry and attempting to finish a novel. She had her first short story, *Winking at Angels*, published in the *Baubles* anthology in 2016. When inspiration dries up, she gazes at the wonderful Snowdon mountain range from her window until it returns.

A Very Unseelie Act

Kate Lowe

To: customerservice@dust-o-matic.com
From: FairyFae@SeelieCourtLeicester.com

Dear Customer Service,

I recently acquired one of your products, the Dust-O-Matic 5000, which was advertised on your website as 'the answer to every busy fairy's prayers'. Said website promised a product that was 'lightweight, dependable and easy to use, with a sprinkle radius of approximately three dandelion stems'. According to the product description, all I had to do was load in the dust, press the button and let the Dust-O-Matic spread the happiness in one easy sweep.

Now, being one of those above-mentioned busy types, I thought the Dust-O-Matic would be ideal for me – no more lugging sacks of dust around, no more trips to the doctor with another case of sprinkle-sprain – and with a thirty percent introductory discount, how could I refuse? On the morning my prized purchase arrived I had a very busy day ahead of me: two weddings to magicate, a driving test to successifize, not to mention the obligatory string of tooth collections and money drops. Great, I thought. This is exactly the kind of day the Dust-O-Matic was made for.

And then I tried to open it.

I would like to challenge you, or any other member of Dust-O-Matic's staff, to get into my 'securely packaged' delivery without the assistance of a pneumatic drill or a blowtorch. I'm sure someone, somewhere, is missing a small forest, and that the inhabitants of a small town or village in a land far, far away are slowly being poisoned by the toxins produced to make the absurd amount of plastic involved in packaging my item!

But I digress.

When I finally got my hands on the Dust-O-Matic, I was dismayed to find that you had not sent the Hot Pink design that I ordered, but something the colour of what is most often found in the nappies of newborn babies. On calling your customer service hotline to report this, I was greeted by an automated call fielding service with more menu options than a Chinese takeaway and a voice like a bridge troll gargling razors. When I eventually got through to the right department, a recorded message advised me that the mailbox was full, in a tone that suggested this was somehow *my* fault, and promptly cut me off.

With the above in mind, please could you arrange for a replacement to be dispatched immediately and advise how I should go about returning the incorrect item?

I look forward to your reply,

Yours Faithfully,

Fae Pepperwood
Seelie Court Fairy Corps, Leicester Branch

~ ~ ~ ~ ~

To: FairyFae@SeelieCourtLeicester.com
From: customerservice@dust-o-matic.com

Dear Pepper,

Thank you for your interest in the Dust-O-Matic brand!
We are sorry to hear that you were disappointed with
your recent purchase. By way of apology, please find
below a printable voucher for ten percent off your next
Dust-O-Matic purchase!

With regards,

Your Dust-O-Matic Team

P.S. Check out our latest model, the Dust-O-Matic 5000
in new Hot Pink!

~ ~ ~ ~ ~

To: customerservice@dust-o-matic.com
From: FairyFae@SeelieCourtLeicester.com

Dear Customer Service,

You clearly did not read my last email properly (copy
attached). Please do so and advise accordingly. Perhaps you
would also be so kind as to take better notice of my name
and not reduce me to a salad vegetable in your reply.

Yours hopefully,

Fae Pepperwood

~~~~~

To: FairyFae@SeelieCourtLeicester.com
From: customerservice@dust-o-matic.com

Dear Fawn,

Thank you for your interest in the Dust-O-Matic brand!
Please find enclosed a copy of our latest catalogue, in
which you will find many exciting and innovative
products, now in a great new Hot Pink range!

With regards,

Your Dust-O-Matic Team

~~~~~

To: customerservice@dust-o-matic.com
From: FairyFae@SeelieCourtLeicester.com

Dear Customer Disservice,

Since you are clearly incompetent I gave up on ever
receiving my Hot Pink model and settled for the Tepid
Sewage design you so kindly foisted on me instead.
Allow me to explain why I now consider this to be the
worst decision I ever made.
On the morning of January 8th I was assigned to attend the
wedding of... well, I won't bother to provide names because
you're not very good with them, are you? The wedding in
question took place in a small village church on a crisp, clear
winter's day. The bride wore white, the groom was ever-so-

slightly inebriated, the guests seemed to be competing in a 'Most Inappropriate Hat' competition – there was nothing, as you can see, out of the ordinary. That is, until I arrived with my Dust-O-Matic 5000.

There I was, hovering behind a fold of the vicar's cassock, waiting to sprinkle a cloud of fairy dust as the final 'I do' was uttered. At the appropriate moment I lifted the Dust-O-Matic, aimed, and pressed the button, expecting a fine mist of fairy dust to envelop the happy couple and give their marital bliss that extra little pep as we Seelie types are wont to do.

Instead, several other things happened all at once.

There was an almighty bang, followed shortly after by a muffled thud and an agonised yell from the groom as he fell to his knees, clutching parts of himself that were soft and delicate. Yes indeed, I had just shot the groom in the unmentionables with a projectile of compacted fairy dust. If only it had stopped there.

The loud bang and subsequent collapse of the groom convinced the congregation they were under attack. Questionable headgear askew, they scattered from the pews like swarming scarab beetles scouting for dung. Admirably, the bride stayed to attend to her injured husband-to-be, as did the vicar, who had no sooner stooped to offer his assistance than the damned Dust-O-Matic went off in my hand again. The vicar straightened like a flick knife, clutching himself in parts that a vicar shouldn't be clutching himself in, at which point the bride let out a scream that brought both mothers-in-law running to the scene.

Stampeding mothers-in-law. Can you imagine? Sprightly woodland elves they were not.

In fear of being trampled, I shot backwards and got my wings tangled in the vicar's flapping cassock. Down I went, and as my bottom hit the flagstones the Dust-O-Matic went off again.

And again. And again.

The force of each round – as that's what I had come to think of them as by then – caused me to bounce along the flagstones on my backside, peppering pew, pulpit and a fetching stained glass interpretation of St Peter as I went. In a desperate attempt to get the dratted thing under control, I aimed the misfiring device towards the farther reaches of the church in the hope of avoiding further casualties, but alas, the organist, a rather frail old lady who'd taken all of that time just to get up from her stool, caught one in the face and went down like she'd been clotheslined.

I won't bore you with further details, and quite honestly I'd much rather forget the whole affair. Needless to say the wedding was ruined, and based on the anatomy your inept piece of tat shot the groom in, I'm guessing that the honeymoon wasn't much fun either. The vicar is managing to sit down now, albeit with the use of a rubber ring, and the organist's fractured jaw is healing nicely, although ingesting her food through a straw must be somewhat tedious.

I have now reached a natural point in this missive in which to call for some kind of response from you, but as I realise that is unlikely to happen I have instead forwarded my complaint to the relevant ombudsman who should be in touch with you in due course. I would like to end by commending you on a simply astonishing display of incompetence, and to thank you for teaching me a very good lesson: if something ain't broke, don't fix it! I'm looking forwards to the sprinkle-sprain already.

Yours wearily,

Fae Pepperwood,

~ ~ ~ ~ ~

To: FairyFae@SeelieCourtLeicester.com
From: MarieMcFlea@SeelieCourtHQ.com

Dear Private Pepperwood,

It has come to our attention that on the 8th January of this year you did attend an assignment, the wedding of one Mr James Smith to Miss Melody Jones, at which you were tasked with magicating the nuptials by means of fairy dust. Not only did the magication fail to take place, Mr Smith, along with several others in attendance, did receive various soft tissue injuries and suffered severe mental trauma that we have reason to believe were delivered by the fairy in attendance.
This was a very Unseelie act and one that this Court will not tolerate. Please be advised that your employment with the Seelie Court, Leicester Branch, has been terminated with immediate effect. If you wish to challenge this decision, please find enclosed a copy of the appeals procedure.

Yours in disappointment,

Marie McFlea, Seelie Court President

Seelie Court! Proud to be sponsored by Dust-O-Matic!

~ ~ ~ ~ ~

To: GrizeldaTumbleweed@UnseelieCourtHQ.com
From: FaePep@GenMail.com

Dear Grizelda,

Please find enclosed my CV in support of my application
to join the Unseelie Court.

I look forwards to hearing from you,

Fae Pepperwood

~ ~ ~ ~ ~

To: FaePep@GenMail.com
From: GrizeldaTumbleweed@UnseelieCourtHQ.com

Dear Fae,

I very much enjoyed meeting with you today. I am
pleased to confirm an offer of employment with the
Unseelie Court. If you wish to accept our offer please
complete the attached paperwork and return to
Unseelie HQ.

I look forwards to working with you,

Grizelda Tumbleweed., Unseelie Court President

~ ~ ~ ~ ~

To: customerservice@dust-o-matic.com
From: FairyFae@UnseelieCourtLeicester.com

Dear Customer Service,
Be seeing you shortly. I will bring the Dust-O-Matic.

Fae Pepperwood

About the author
Kate Lowe is the author of the urban fantasy series *The Riley Pope Case Files*. Her work has appeared in several anthologies, and her story *The Wolf Runs in the Barley* received an Honourable Mention in "The Best Horror of the Year Volume 4". You can visit her website at www.kateloweauthor.co.uk to find out more.

All That Glitters

Theresa Sainsbury

I remember that Christmas so well. It was my first year in France and I was lonely. Desperately lonely. The language barrier, the strange school system, the frostiness of the French people and the general misery of being a spotty, misunderstood teenager, all seemed to conspire against me.

My salvation was the festive season itself. Shop windows at Christmas promise so much. Their well decorated stage sets remind me of the possibilities of the season. Santa Claus, presents, trees, baubles, glamour and glitter.

But I ignored the big department stores, eschewing their corporate, bland, over coiffured displays, preferring the intimacy and quirkiness of the independent shop owner, who tends to curate a more eclectic look.

I spotted the item purely by chance, deviating from my regular journey home, running an errand for my mother, spinning out the walk so I could daydream, invent new stories, think of ideas in my home tongue and take a rest from the complexities of my new language.

The labyrinth of narrow streets off the main thoroughfare are my favourite routes. And Paris delights in these narrow winding boulevards as much as it does with the small specialist shops that inhabit them. The city seems able to support this more dedicated purveyor of gifts, where time stands still and as the shop door opens the customer is treated not only to a visual feast but the knowledge that they are in the safe hands of an expert.

I'd passed Maison du Stylo before, but it had been raining, one of those heavy, biting winter showers that chases all but the hardiest off the streets, so I had rushed past, making a mental note of the location and promising myself a return trip.

And now I was back. I took time to enjoy the exterior, before venturing inside. First, I examined the old-fashioned lettering on the shop hoarding, an attractive vintage typeface that I couldn't place, but contained hints of a highly decorative calligraphy, black on a gold background, making it the perfect choice. The windows themselves looked original, edged in ageing wood, wrapping around the front of the building into the recessed door of the shop itself, providing an extended podium to display the wares. The tiled porchway was well worn, uneven, dirtied by the numerous customers venturing in and out, attracted just like I was.

And the wares; where to start? Montblanc, Tiffany, Parker, Cello, the list goes on. But more than that was the sheer beauty of it all. Charming wooden display units with glossy, glass tops and slim drawers, pulled out halfway to show beautiful instruments in a range of complimentary colours. Interspersed amongst these were wooden beakers, plain silver cups with pens arranged vertically, providing height to the display. In front of each container was a thick piece of manuscript paper covered in beautiful cursive script, with a single pen, its top removed, laid down at the side, as if the author was taking a quick break and would be back any minute. A piece of papyrus lay next to an elegant quill and a tiny inkpot with a short phrase scratched out delicately across its surface; I translated it slowly in my head "This is how it started," followed by two artfully placed ink spots. A dash of humour.

The display cleverly drew my eyes from its idiosyncratic edges to the centre, where there was a distinct nod to the festive season. A large rectangle of expensive-looking paper was set in a vintage silver frame. The paper was covered with a delicate frosting of silver glitter and in Forte type face I spotted the words to 'Silent Night'. Somehow the French translation sounded more romantic, 'Nuit Silencieux'. At times like this, away from the stress and strain of the classroom, I learnt to love my new language. In an open box, centre right to the frame, completing the triad of silver, was the pen of my dreams. A Montblanc Meisterstuck Royal Solitaire White Diamond; an elegant glittering device, studded with masses and masses of tiny expensive jewels and gilded with a flourish of eighteen carat gold. I took a sharp intake of breath. Felt the trace of a smile on my lips. I'd seen pictures, but never been this close to a real one. No price tag, none needed, it was worth as much as a small apartment!

The door jangled as I went in and a woody aroma greeted me, with the faintest hint of something slightly aromatic just below the surface. Ink. The shopkeeper was busy with a customer, so I made my way slowly around the glass topped cabinets. I'd found my own proverbial sweet shop.

I suppose I must have looked out of place, a skinny fifteen-year-old girl schoolgirl, clearly lacking the spending power that an establishment like this required, but the shopkeeper was kind and indulgent and spent half an hour with me that particular day discussing pens and allowing my shaking hand to pick up the Solitaire.

My love of writing instruments had developed out of a fascination for writing. And I mean writing, not the tap, tap, tap of a keyboard. There is something exciting about the act of moving a well-constructed pen across paper to produce a unique script. Something that identifies me, defines me. And of course, the Montblanc represented the pinnacle of all pens. A glittery, ostentatious glorious dazzler of a pen!

I changed my route home from school, got into the habit of passing Maison du Stylo every afternoon in December. Paused and looked longingly at the beautiful glittering object in the window. In my dreams, I owned it.

Then on 23 December, I had the dream.

The pen was in my hand and I was writing as I'd never written before. A Mystery. A girl trapped in someone else's story.

She ran faster and faster. She knew she was trying to escape from someone or something. Panting heavily. Footsteps were thumping after her, the streetlights snapped off, providing a few seconds' respite to make a quick decision. She turned sharply into a doorway, leant tight against the front door, her body flattening out, extending, feeling every tiny protrusion and indentation behind her. The sound of the footsteps faded. She glanced left to right and realised the door belonged to a shop and as she peeled her body away, the entry gave way behind her. "Come in" someone whispered seductively. A soft light shone inside, bathing the interior in a comforting glow. The girl felt a sense of relief, as if the fear and tension had retreated the minute she crossed the threshold. There was an oak table in the centre of the room with a sensible upright wooden chair behind it. The table bore a lamp, a sheaf of paper and sparkling in the light, catching it at every angle, was a diamond encrusted pen. The voice spoke again, "Sit, relax, you are safe. Read the story that someone else has started and if you devise the correct ending, the pen is yours."

I heard my voice interjecting, "But I'm writing this story," I said confused, "And I already have the diamond pen in my hand."

"Ah, but your story is only half the puzzle," said the voice. "Your character needs to finish the one started by someone else to prove beyond doubt your worth as a writer."

The girl seemed oblivious to this little exchange and sat down in the chair and looked around her. There was no doubt that she was in a shop; a pen shop. On every available surface and peering out of every glass cabinet were pens. Different colours, brands, prices, types. Fountain pens, ball point pens, refills, nibs, boxes, cases, cartridges and bottles of ink. All this paraphernalia reinforced her feeling of security, so she picked up the diamond encrusted pen and wrote. She didn't bother to read the half a page of script that already covered the paper, she just took note of the last line; *Ruby was lonely, friendless and her parents had no time for her.*

The girl had a wonderful hand; the pen moved gracefully across her writing surface with loops and lines emerging effortlessly. She made fast progress, pausing every now and then to consider an idea, a word, casting a glance around the room, checking her surroundings, drawing confidence it seemed from the ambience.

After three pages, she stopped, adding her final caesura with a flourish.

"You've finished," said the phantom voice, more as a command than a question. The girl inclined her head.

"What happened to your character, to Ruby?" The girl lifted the sheets of paper to the light, arms outstretched, looking much like a priest at the altar, whilst I gazed on, unable to speak.

The voice read out the final lines of the story.

Ruby clutched the diamond pen in her hand, almost as if she was squeezing the life out of it. She realised the instrument had no magic powers, endowed no skill that could not be gained from a pencil or cheap biro. She put it back in its box and snapped it shut. She had not written well with it. Perhaps she was too much in awe of it, perhaps she was simply dazzled by its beauty, diverted by its glamour?

She picked up her pencil, the short stubby one with the chewed end, and resumed her work.

The voice paused, the girl withdrew her arms, placed the paper back on the table. She made a movement to sit down, but never got there. She disappeared. Evaporated. The pen sparkled on the table.

I was aware that I still had the same pen in my hand. Feelings of anxiety bubbled.

The voice spoke for the last time. "You don't need the pen. It glitters, but the lustre will fade. You would soon tire of it."

I remember throwing the pen, feeling a sudden need to get rid of it as quickly as possible, but I never saw it fall.

On Christmas Eve, there was no school, but after lunch I wandered the streets nonetheless, glad to be out of our cramped apartment as I'd spent all morning writing and needed a change of scene. I felt compelled to go to Maison du Stylo, but made a promise to myself that it would be my last visit. The obsession with the diamond pen needed to end. At the window, I realised something was different; the Christmas display in the centre, the frame, the glitter, the pen, had been dismantled and there was just a gaping hole where the items had once been. Before I had time to think, the door jangled open. "Bonjour! Entrez" entreated the shop owner.

The same smell, the same aromatic undertone. The owner had retreated behind the counter and returned with a slim rectangular box. He gestured to me to take it. I opened it and inside was a stainless-steel Parker Pen, a solid, sensible, dependable writing instrument and as I removed it from the box, the light caught it, glinting and shining defiantly. There was a card in the lid of the box which simply said "To the young lady who loves writing. All that glitters".

About the author
Theresa is an avid reader and writer, currently working as a private tutor in Richmond Upon Thames, specialising in hauling teenagers through the demands of GCSE English Language and Literature. She has two children of her own who both prefer Science to the Arts, and her husband programmes computers and will only read books with a number in the title! Theresa writes every day and enjoys every single second of it.

Brighter Than Jewels

Gail Aldwin

"How did you meet Mel?" Ellie asks. A speck of chocolate on her top lip remains from the sprinkles on her cappuccino. With her eyelids marked in a sweep of italic liner, she looks older than sixteen years. Only the fleck gives her youth away. "What're you staring at?"

"You've got something on your lip." I point to the spot on my face, where the mark appears on my daughter's. She licks a napkin and dabs.

"Gone?" She juts her chin forwards.

"Not quite. I've got a mirror in my bag."

"Don't worry. I'm going to the loo. I'll sort it." Ellie pushes back the chair, scraping the slate floor of the cafe's veranda.

"The toilet's down those stairs." I nod my head in the general direction. She takes a few strides then step by step, she disappears from sight. Releasing a sigh, my shoulders relax. It's hard work being with her sometimes.

Staff wearing full-length aprons distribute menus around the tables in preparation for the dinner service. The paper flaps in the swirl of air from the ceiling fans. Most of the afternoon tea customers have left and I realise I've stayed too long. I catch the attention of a waiter and he brings the bill on a saucer. He waits while I rummage through my wallet to find a blue dollar note and pass it over.

"Keep the change," I say, even though it's not usual to tip in Australia.

I'm waiting on the path when Ellie appears, she smirks at my hat. It's not the greatest design, monochrome stripes but at least it's protection from the sun. I like the warmth in Cairns, heat that gets right into my bones but Ellie's

31

suffering. Her nose is covered in freckles and there are beads of sweat on her forehead.

"Let's go down to the lagoon – I've brought a towel so we can paddle." I nudge her arm but she backs away.

"What's the point? I haven't got a swimsuit. And I don't even own one that fits properly."

"Shall we stop at the mall? See if there's anything that'll suit you?"

"Okay," she says. "You do realise I'm going to fail my maths module."

"No, why should you? You've brought your revision books."

"But I've missed the last week of term and I'll never understand the new work they've covered."

"I'm sure it'll be all right. Besides, there's not much I can do about it now. Let's try and enjoy the holiday."

"Fine. As long as you know the consequences."

"Yes." I know the consequences absolutely.

Ellie frowns but falls into step as I take the lead. We follow a route through the grid of streets that brings us to the mall. It's strange that I still know my way after all these years. Not that the shopping mall existed then, but Mel told me it was tacked onto the back of the railway station and I get my bearings from there. The building's vast, covers an entire block, brick built and gable roofed. Not one window open, not even a glass-fronted display. I push the revolving door and immediately I'm chilled. The air conditioning springs the hairs on my arms to attention and I unravel the sleeves pushed to my elbows. Inside gangs of girls wearing very short shorts, sip frozen juice through straws and take to the aisles as if working a catwalk. Boys skulk by the benches, a thicket of arms and legs as they lark about. I notice Ellie's dismissive glances, clearly it's not how her friends behave.

"So how did you meet Mel?" Ellie tries again.

"We were both here on a working holiday and we shared a room at the backpackers' hostel."

"Why d'you stay in a hostel?"

"We were travelling on a budget, like gap year students, only I wasn't destined for university."

"Why not?"

"Back then a girls' secondary school education gave a pass into the workplace then marriage. Nothing more."

"But you got married in Australia, didn't you?" She frowns as she talks. "The first time."

"That's right. In fact I got married here in Cairns."

"You never told me that. Where d'you get married?"

"In Rusty's Bazaar, down in Grafton Street."

"Can we take a look?"

"Of course, but let's see about the swimming stuff while we're here."

I'm tired of the grilling and head into a shop where the display shows tiny bikini pants suspended on silver threads. I grasp the fabric. It slithers through my fingers and I pull the embroidered edge to inspect the pattern of sequins. Ellie's at the back of the shop, looking at the two-piece sets made from darker material. When I approach, she's holding a hanger where a purple bikini top bulges with padding. The poor girl's so flat-chested, I wonder she hasn't asked for a boob-job as a Christmas present.

"That's a nice colour," I say.

"Shall I try it on?"

"Okay." I nod. "But how about this one?" I show her my choice; she gives it a cursory glance.

"I don't think much of the flashy beads."

"As you like."

"You try it on. It'll look good on you."

"No, I only go in for costumes these days."

33

I give Ellie five minutes then go to find her in the changing room. Poking my head around the curtain I see Ellie struggling into her jeans, her limbs made awkward by the denim bunched around her knees. Before I have time to speak, she yanks the curtain closed and I stare at the warped threads. I tell Ellie I'll meet her by the cash register and return to the glare of the shop. Browsing the silky thongs as I wander through, I imagine the discomfort of wearing one. Ellie appears with a smile wide enough to concede that she's pleased with the try-on. I ask the assistant to remove the labels and she packs the purchase.

We detour by the hotel so Ellie can change, the straps of the bikini show under the oversized T-shirt that falls off her shoulders, the frayed hem reaching almost past the turn-ups on her shorts. I like the way Ellie struts, showing the confidence I never had.

"Can we go to Rusty's Bazaar?" Ellie asks.

"Not now – it's a fruit market – only worth visiting in the mornings."

"You got married in a fruit market?"

"It was more of a craft market then."

"Even so," she sneers. "Surely you could have done better than that."

"You're not wrong there, and the bloke wasn't much good either."

"Why d'you marry him?"

"I was broke and lonely and a long way from home." We stop at a pedestrian crossing and wait for the lights to change. The road is quiet, we could've chanced it. Ellie frowns. "Don't look at me like that. I've always been upfront with you. You knew I had a husband before I married Dad. It's no big deal. I just made a mistake."

"Err Mrs Edwards," she speaks into her curled fingers like a microphone. "Just explain why it's necessary to visit

34

the town of your err, big mistake." Grabbing her elbow, I tug Ellie across the road as if she's a naughty toddler. She giggles at my embarrassment and pulls away. A strand of blonde hair dangles over her eyes. I size up to her, ready for a confrontation.

"My personal history's nothing to laugh at. It just happens to be a coincidence that Mel lives here. And I wasn't going to travel all this way without seeing her, repaying the compliment if you like." I'm in full flow now, justifying my very existence. "She always comes to stay with us when she visits her folks in London and it seemed logical to spend a few days here before meeting up with Dad in Sydney."

"Okay, Mum. Calm down."

"You could've stayed with Dad in Hong Kong if you really didn't want to come."

"Just chill, won't you? God. I only asked a question." She folds her arms.

"I'm sorry. Jet-lag makes me short tempered. Come on, let's get down to the water."

Slapping the pavement with her feet in flip-flops, Ellie walks ahead of me. The sky is turning to lavender and bats head for cover. The trees are alive with screeches, dangling black outlines visible amongst the leaves. Ducking as a bat swoops, Ellie squeals and retraces her steps. She loops her arm though mine and we walk on, clinging together, her bony hip bumps against mine and we giggle at our fright. I like having her close to me.

We circle the man-made lagoon, underwater lights show the bathers' legs in silhouettes, their bodies sparkling with droplets above the water line. Children play with toy boats in the shallows. Over by the picnic benches, parents gather, half-watching the activity in the water and waiting for the arrival of dinner from the barbecue. Smoke

35

wafts and flames dart through the grills. Wielding cooking tongs, the men in aprons spar and the smell of charred meat emanates. My rumbling stomach reminds me it's time to meet Mel and my watch shows it's gone seven o'clock, she'll be waiting at the pizza place. I tell Ellie we should leave, that there's no time for swimming but we can paddle. I slip barefoot into the ankle deep water. I swirl my legs and with each step, enjoy the splatter along my calves. Ellie watches, deciding whether to join me and then she follows my progress. It's warm enough not to bother drying my legs and I thread my toes through the sandal straps.

Sitting at a table beside the road, Mel studies the menu. Curly hair screens her face as she stares at the writing. She startles as we approach, Ellie settles into the empty chair opposite and I take the one in the middle.

"You gave me a fright." Mel taps her heart.

"I remember you scare easily. Always ripe for a practical joke."

"Don't remind me." Mel turns to look at me, a flicker of a memory catches us.

"It's a good job that low-flying ashtray missed you. You could've been decapitated had you moved in the wrong direction."

"What happened?" Ellie asks.

"Oh, it was just a disagreement with the boss where we worked," I say.

"Doesn't do to criticise a pub manager," Mel says. "Even if he's an arsehole."

Ellie sniggers.

"Have you decided what to order?" I ask.

"There's only one veggie thing on the menu. Guess it's a Margarita for me."

"Why did the manager try to kill you?" Ellie asks.

"Had a bit of a short fuse did Barry. But I don't suppose calling his prize pub-lunch a school dinner helped much."

"Least said about that the better," I say.

"The man was a nutter," Mel continues. "Dabbled in too many magic mushrooms."

"A sixth former at my school was expelled for possession of hash."

"What?" I say. "You mean he took drugs into school?"

"Yeah." Ellie smiles. "Bit of a dealer. He offered to sell me some."

"I hope you said no."

"Of course, told him I wasn't interested." I let out a sigh of relief and Ellie continues. "Directed him to the skaters, they'd smoke anything. They even tried to smoke some of Dad's parsley at my party last summer. That's why all the boys were squashed into the greenhouse."

"I thought they'd gone in there for shelter when it started raining."

"As if," says Ellie.

The pizzas arrive and I rearrange the table to accommodate the plates. The wine glasses chink together and I need a refill. Already the bottle's half empty, but Mel shakes her head as I offer more and Ellie's hardly touched hers. I pour the white nearly to the rim; the glass runs with condensation. It's years since I've enjoyed an evening meal outside when I haven't been swathed in blankets. It's liberating to be in summer clothes, especially as it's winter back home. I could do this every year, I reflect.

With a pile of discarded olives on the side of her plate, Ellie bites into the last slice of pizza, her scratched fingernails show patches of apricot varnish. I chase the salad leaves around the bowl and spear a piece of cucumber. My appetite appeased, I lean against the backrest and I notice my stomach bulge under the napkin. I gulp the breeze as it flaps hair around my shoulders and I tune into the notes of a lone saxophone player in the distance.

"Were you with my mum when she got married?" Ellie puts her elbows on the table, resting her chin on her palm.

"No, was off working on a prawn trawler by then. It was all done and dusted by the time I got back. Funny that." Mel finishes a forkful and chews.

"It was all such a long time ago, Ellie. There's no point in having a Spanish Inquisition."

"Jesus, Mum. I'm just curious. Why on earth did you get married?"

"Well, it wasn't just to get Australian Residency like Mel."

"What? You got married, too?" Ellie's jaw drops.

"A year in the sun and I never wanted to go home. Married one of the customers from the pub but it all went pear-shaped within a few months. I got a job on the trawler and we didn't see each other for years. He tracked me down when he wanted a divorce."

"You make it sound easy," said Ellie.

"It was. But your mum's experience was different. She met Dale in the pub too. But he spun her a tale of sailing the South Pacific Islands and living off barter."

"Barter?"

"Dale planned to exchange his skills for food and beer. Had this crazy idea that there'd be a need for a western chef on islands where they do little more than light a fire to cook their meals," I say. "But he made it sound so possible, so reasonable. And there was Mel off on the prawn trawler, what else was I to do but marry him?"

"It wasn't my fault you married him." Mel turns to face me, a frown scoring her brow. "It's not as if I didn't warn you. Told you all that talk of love and poetry was nonsense."

"I know, I know. Call me gullible. And before you ask, Ellie, I never did set sail. Dale had a brainwave that we should go to Sydney. That he'd find work there – get a decent job. Then perhaps we could join a cruise, rather than a do-it-yourself tour of the islands."

"Is that why we're going to Sydney next? To retrace your steps?"

"Of course not."

The town is emptying by the time we leave the restaurant, a couple of back-packers zig-zag the pavement, struggling under the weight of the bags. Ellie swings her arm beside mine and our knuckles brush. We pass a pub with its doors swung open, the staff rearranging chairs and washing glasses. I recognise the crocodile of carved wood that decorates the length of the bar, the tail-end where Dale stood to order beer. I stop on the corner where the smokers spilt onto the street in the early hours, me amongst them. Walking another block, I find the motel where we stayed for a month, waiting for the marriage licence to be issued. We slept in a creaking double and I used a shower that dropped pins of water over my pink flesh. I notice the peeling weatherboard and I remember the time Dale made an entrance through the window like Romeo, by climbing the planks. I stifle a giggle by turning it into a cough and Ellie slaps my back. Around the corner there's the bench, the one where we had our photograph taken. The picture marked the day of our wedding, when I wore jeans and Dale admired my bridal outfit. Further along I linger outside the post office, where I sent the letter telling my parents of the marriage and the poste restante where I waited for their reply.

"Why've we stopped?" Ellie asks.

"Take a look at the stars."

39

Ellie angles her head. "Wish I had a diamond ring that size."

"Memories are brighter than jewels, Ellie."

"If you say so, Mum."

About the author

Gail Aldwin is a prize-winning writer of flash fiction, short stories, and poetry. Her work can be found online at *Ink, Sweat & Tears* and *Slamchop* and in print anthologies including *What I Remember* (EVB Press, 2015) *Dorset Voices* (Roving Press, 2012) and *The Last Word* (Unbound Press, 2012). Gail writes collaboratively with other women to develop comedy for the screen and stage. With the Dorset Writers' Network, Gail supports isolated writers in rural areas. She is an experienced teacher who delivers workshops to young people and adults in community settings. You can find Gail @gailaldwin and http://gailaldwin.wordpress.com.

Her Coronet Weeds

Yasmina Floyer

Is the sea angry? Ophelia asks, hugging her knees to her chest. The cold roof tiles numb her little bottom and the backs of her legs. Her toes feel alien to her in soggy socks, fingers asleep in redundant gloves. When her father, who sits beside her, asks whether she is cold, she says no, absentmindedly kicking the heels of her trainers together. The flashing lights in the rubber heel stopped working long ago. She itches at her shock of red hair, usually immaculate in plaited pigtails, now an unruly of tangle curls. It had always been mother's job to brush it.

Her eyes are fixed on a magpie floating in the briny floodwater. Steam rises in spite of the impending cold brought on by the evening. The bird's once monochrome plume has amalgamated into a xanthous hue, similar to the sun-bleached fur of Ophelia's teddies, mottled and neglected on her bedroom windowsill. A rainbow film on the skin of the water's surface parts reverentially to allow the bird passage toward the crumbling bricks of Ophelia's house and for a moment she is able to forget as the magpie cuts through the spectrum of colour. Moments later the noxious film disperses and seagulls circle overhead.

It takes a while for her to realise that the bird is dead, that it is the current of the water and nothing more compelling it to bob against the side of the house before pulling away and bobbing against it once more. The magpie tilts towards her to expose a featherless wing, its tiny bones like spindly crochet needles. Her father, noticing the object of his daughter's gaze, wraps an arm around her shoulders. She squirms beneath his hold, all angles jutting into his ribs until she produces a copper penny from her sock. She holds

41

it up so close to her father's face that he can smell the bloody warmth of it.

It has my birthday on it, Daddy, she says, holding it closer still. Ophelia holds it tightly in her fist then flicks it high. The ring of the coin cleanses the air before landing with a low slap. She watches the red fade, then disappear, looking hard at the water until she is certain it is gone. The girl waits to see what the coin will bring up but is met with nothing but a widening ring of ripples that eventually reaches the side of the house, agitating the magpie.

A few days ago, the rain came and stayed. The wind was next. Ophelia wriggled in Margot's lap as her mother teased out stubborn knots. The two of them paid little attention to the blurring image on the television screen. It was the same on every channel: another week of rain and wind snapping electrical pylons like ligaments, paralysing small coastal towns like theirs. The news reporter's voice cut in and out but 'no immediate risk' managed to filter through.

Why does Daddy only come home on the weekend now? Ophelia was met with the static hiss of the hair brush, tugging her head back in sharp jolts. She braced herself for yelling, except this time it didn't come. Her hair crackled in the close air. No yelling and somehow Ophelia knew this was worse. Now, eat your breakfast, Margot said. A single wheat biscuit fattening in a bowl of warm water. Ophelia didn't miss the milk. She knew it would come later with her father along with a small packet of meat wrapped tightly in brown paper.

Margot strained the teabag that barely tinted the water and decided this time to throw it out. The reporter's voice came in clearly to say that there was no immediate threat to coastal towns. No immediate threat, she repeated to herself and kept her eyes on the shifting platelets of lime scale in her teacup, watching the work of millennia in fast motion; the forming and reforming of plate tectonics in miniature. She imagined the tea rising up and over the brim of chipped china. No immediate threat, she thought, picking at the hardening callous that had been forming in the hollow of her knee, picking at it to get to the smooth beneath.

Margot waited until her daughter was done scraping her bowl clean, watched her mouth spoonfuls of nothing to make certain there was nothing more to be had. You know full well why your father comes home on weekends only, she said, he works very hard to take care of us. She managed not to scoff on saying this. Ophelia searched her mother's face for more but nothing more came. Margot told her that he will be home very soon. What she didn't say is that her father doesn't want to come back but that he always does. She didn't tell her that during the weeks, he isn't Lonely Daddy or Poor Daddy, that he kisses another child on the head goodnight, a son, not much older than herself. She didn't need to know that he got into bed at night with the boy's mother, who was not her own mother, and that when they lie together, on those nights Margot felt it in her blood and howled into her pillow to deaden the sound.

The rain water came into the kitchen through generous crevices like an uninvited guest, darkening the carpet. The wind had whipped the sea up, pushing it well beyond the shore, the excesses of which collected unevenly at the back of the cottage where the house slumped into its foundations. Each year the rain came, the walls remained saturated from within like a disease, black spores cultivating in the corners of the room, spreading across the walls like ink into blotting paper. This year the sea pulled out farther than before and Margot knew it would not go back until it had what belonged to it.

Margot no longer bothered with rubber gloves. She scrubbed at the walls, scratches on her knuckles rankled by the neat bleach she no longer bothered to dilute, waiting for him to return. He is late again, she thought, each weekend he is getting later and later. The heady solution went to work on the skin of hands and the soles of her feet, creating a lacework pattern of little holes. She imagined these holes expanding with time eating away and leaving her completely bare. She did not bother to cream her palms, making them smooth to touch. She had not needed to bother with that for quite some time. He will come back today, she told herself. He will come, he will come, he will come, and she kept telling herself until all that was left were patchy yellow stains where the mould had been.

He called Margot his remedy, told her she was intoxicating. She pretended not to notice him when he woke on the beach at dawn abandoned by his stag party, still drunk from the night before. He thought the russet blaze on the horizon was the sun. Rubbing away the sand imbedded onto his cheek, what he took for the sun became red hair loose and long, blanketing Margot's face and her nakedness as she bent low to pick limpets from rocks, sucking them out live. He sat shivering, barely noticing the cold as he wondered how she was able to walk like that across the rocks without slipping.

She smiled at him when he spoke to her, waiting for the sounds coming from his mouth to arrange into order. He was repeating himself, that much she could tell, and after a few moments she was able to reply, my name is Margot. They made love that morning in the cavern by the beach. He did not notice her feet then.

He told her she was his remedy on the weekends he stole away from the city to be with her and didn't stop telling her this until her belly began to swell. How is that possible? He asked her, when her belly waxed full within a matter of weeks. You know full well how this happened, she said. He shook his head, as if the gesture alone could make it untrue. He told her he did not love her, yelled it at her, and kept on yelling it. Leave me then, she said. Her hardened navel rippled as the babe within shifted, listening. What will it come out like? He asked. Like us, she said, our baby will be like us. Like you, he said, leaving even though it was the middle of the night.

Margot didn't cry but sat out on the doorstep watching him drive away, rubbing at a protruding lump below her ribcage that she knew to be the baby's foot. Watching the back of his car judder away from her, she knew he would come back because she had woven herself into the warp and weft of him.

He didn't arrive until dinnertime. The wind whistled through the fractures of the house transporting the heady bleach all around the cottage. He kept his shoes on but his feet were steeped in the briny water that mounted upon the carpet and kitchen tiles. That stuff is giving me a headache, he said. Ophelia forgot her hunger and stared at her mother, whose eyes appeared bluer with kohl smudged around them. He did not notice her eyes, his own squeezed shut, fingers pressed against them. Margot lit the stove and unwrapped the brown packet sat on the counter.

She sat with her hands in her lap to the clatter of knives and forks and did not go to the sink until those sounds ceased. She drained a pint of water where she stood, panting a little from the effort. Mummy, will you eat now? Ophelia asked, already knowing the response. It occurred to her that she only remembered seeing her mother eat once. Later, O, I will have something later, she would always say, before filling up water-stained glasses to the brim then drinking them down in a single go, belly swelling.

She only remembered seeing her eat that one time. Ophelia was much smaller then, woken by the wind. At first she thought it was her mother again, howling into her pillow behind a locked door on the nights her father worked away. It was always louder when he left; when her father was home they would argue on the landing in hushed voices, thinking she could not hear, but Ophelia inhaled their words and her lungs grew heavy. She went downstairs and followed wet footprints along the hallway tiles to the kitchen. Her mother never wore shoes, even when she walked the distance to the village or down to the beach whose dunes reached the front of their house. Bare wet prints led to the kitchen. Her mother stood looking out of the window; a silver fish on the counter by the sink, moonlight whitening its marble eyes. Ophelia saw her mother pick up the fish without looking, taking a large bite from its side, undeterred by the scales that she mashed in her mouth along with small bones, then wiping the plummy fish blood with the back of her hand, she began to scale and gut the fish.

Are you not hungry, Mummy? Later O, I will eat later. Ophelia left them to play upstairs. The headache had moved to his eye sockets and down still to his jaw. Margot walked over and stood in front of him, her bare feet sloshing in the rising water. For the first time he noticed the small bulge of Margot's stomach and knew it was more than the water she had been drinking. He could not work out if it was his headache creating the illusion of movement along Margot's small mound. That is not possible, Margot, how? The pain moved further down into the roots of his teeth, the closer she got to him the deeper it grew. Gulls screeched above them whipped by the wind. He pointed to her stomach with his fork, and then at once the headache spread to his blood, the searing pain giving him knowledge: Margot lying with another man. She watched her steak adjust to room temperature, its lukewarm blood leaching outwards in spidery rivulets before coming together in a scarlet hale that framed the untouched meat.

Ophelia sat crossed legged on her mother's bed, scraping her nail along the sides of her creations; frangible houses fashioned out of mismatched plastic bricks. Her hair still smelled of fried meat and she chewed the ends as she played. She inspected her constructions with the forensic analysis only capable of child, running a nail along the side of one house, nodding each time it passed a gap where the bricks were joined. Her parents had moved to the landing failing to keep their voices hushed. Stray words slipped beneath the door: tired, witch, hate. Her mother came in and closed the door firmly behind her. Stood in the fading light of the window, Margot removed her makeup holding a cracked plastic mirror. The white wipe took on sooty skin tones until her eyes receded into her skull, hollow without the dark outline, her translucent skin a veiny blue around her jaw, time etched finely around her eyes and across her forehead.

She sat next to Ophelia and picked at the building blocks. Mummy's house and Daddy's house, Ophelia presented. Margot's hand jerked forward a fraction, a micro-gesture promising tenderness and then rested back onto the duvet. But Ophelia already noticed and just like that her mother started to slip away.

The room was black when she woke up. What she believed to be her mother's hand on her cheek was a toy bear she had fallen asleep on. Her houses were dismantled into little bricks again and she could not remember doing that. The house felt still without the incessant hiss where the rain beat down. Ophelia walked out onto the landing and found her father sat against the wall with his head on his knees. The water had crept halfway up the staircase. Ophelia stood at the top of the stairs. Mummy? She called out, rousing her father awake. The house dripped and echoed in response.

He watched her staring down into the water and didn't move from where he was sat until Ophelia began to descend the steps calling after her mother. Scooping her up in one arm, he brought her back to the top of the stairs. His head was clear, his body felt cool. She's gone, he told her, repeating this as Ophelia howled with a depth he had not heard. He held her close, sleeves still damp up to the elbows.

The crescent moon marks a clean thumbnail in the sky, washed in lemony hues by the setting sun. Ophelia watches its ascent from the roof as it rises behind bare trees that create a silhouette of bone dry lungs. Her father is repeating himself, telling her again about her new life in the city and the brother she has not yet met. He is not much older than you, you know?

Ophelia ignores her father and watches the water's surface, imagining her mother is not gone but changed somehow, smaller and living in one of her plastic houses. In the dying light she sees movement below. Her father follows her gaze staring deep into the placid liquid, seeing nothing but the quavering sickle of the moon's reflection. He looks to his daughter and asks, what is it, O? Nothing, she replies at the red plume wafting towards the surface. A flash of silver licks the skin of the water, scattering the sickle moon into specs of white. Nothing, she says, rubbing at the callous forming on the skin of her calf, rubbing hard to get to the smooth below.

About the author
Yasmina lives in London where she takes care of her family and works as a private tutor. Since completing a Master's in Creative Writing at Glasgow University, her work has been published in Avis Literary Journal, Litro Magazine and the forthcoming *Twenty-Four Stories Anthology* in aid of the Grenfell Tower survivors. Her poems are published online at By&By Poetry.

Kitsune

David Trebus

Dominic opened his eyes to darkness. Small shafts of moonlight helped illuminate the gloom as he looked around. Large tree trunks surrounded him in all directions. *A forest? How did you find yourself in a forest, genius?*

Dominic tried to stand, his legs protesting at the effort. He winced as a sharp pain hit his temple. He staggered, fetching up against a tree trunk. Odd. The sensation faded as quickly as it had appeared, like a muscle memory of something unpleasant long since passed.

Dominic quickly regained his footing, taking a few steps away from the tree. Nothing around him seemed familiar. No signs, no clear paths, and no road nearby to follow back to civilization. A sick sensation settled in Dominic's stomach. This was not good, anything could have happened.

"Mobile…"

His jeans' pockets held house keys, a wrist watch missing half a strap and a wallet. The watch was frozen at 9:15pm, with the hands refusing to move. He patted his sweater, then his jacket feeling the familiar shape of his smartphone in one of the many pockets. The screen glowed but refused to respond. It seemed to be jammed.

"Hitsuzen." An unknown number appeared on the top of the screen.

The text brought another sharp stab to his temple. Wincing, Dominic felt a wet sensation running down the back of his neck. His hand shot up to check but there was nothing there, just the same short brown hair he had always had. No wet patches, no pain. It disappeared again as quickly as it came on.

Pressing the buttons did nothing to unjam the phone. It refused to respond, the same strange text on the glowing screen. Dominic pocketed it. *What the Hell did Hitsuzen mean anyway?*

For now, the priority had to be finding a way back, but to where? He couldn't remember. He recalled his name, he knew he was twenty-six, he knew his parents' names and address. He couldn't remember where he lived, or what he was doing in a forest in the middle of the night.

There had to be a house close by to make a call from or at least a road to follow. He started walking, picking a random direction. *What if I never find my way back?* Dominic staggered as waves of dislocation washed over him. He fetched up against a tree trunk.

Dominic turned his eyes to the way ahead. Leaves crunched beneath his feet as he trudged forwards. It was difficult to see their colours in the twilight but it had to be autumn by the number of leaves on the ground.

Staying focussed on walking eased the tides of anxiety. Each crunching step returned him to the world. Looking up Dominic saw more gaps in the trees' canopy. Stars shone above, winking at him through the holes. Stumbling, Dominic's attention returned to the forest. The ground was paved.

"Finally!" Dominic couldn't help but yell out in relief.

A paved path extended up a hill towards a distant building and round a corner leading out of sight. The path upwards was lit by burning sconces, hanging from large red painted archways. The building in the distance glowed with warm light, likely a porch light or more sconces.

The path leading down could lead to a village or a main roadway but between the two options going towards the light always seemed like a good option. *Unless you're in that movie Poltergeist.*

After the uneven forest ground, the paving stones were

much easier to navigate. Dominic strode up the hill like an athlete in training, the previous weakness in his muscles completely faded. *Was that normal?* Dominic put it down to adrenaline and the easier footing.

Stone reliefs watched over the path at regular intervals during his ascent. Each was carved in the shape of a fox or other vulpine creature. Some had scarves tied around their necks, others burned out candles set at their feet. Dominic remembered reading about Japanese culture and foxes being revered as deities. He reached out, brushing his hand against one.

A fox? Images exploded in Dominic's mind. A name repeated over and over: *Anna?*

A brief view of a plane flashed, then a sign: Tokyo International Airport. Then a hotel room and a play fight with pillows; Anna always lost on purpose. Finally, a car and a smiling farewell, then… The pain became overwhelming, so much so, Dominic felt he was going to black out.

He clenched his fist around the fox statue's large stone muzzle and squeezed his eyes shut, trying to focus on his breathing. "Please God, let this stop. What's happening? Help me!"

The pain stopped as abruptly as it had begun. Instead of fading, it was as if it had never even been. Dominic steadied himself and patted the statue. *Someone's listening to my prayers.*

The headaches were unnerving, but at least he remembered fragments now. He knew he was likely on a trip with someone called Anna in Japan. It went a long way to explaining the large red archways and stone statues. The exact details of his predicament would hopefully come back in time.

Dominic resumed his climb, stepping across the threshold of the final archway into a small courtyard. At least fifty statues surrounded him there. They stared with cold marble eyes, firelight dancing within obsidian orbs. The building itself looked like some kind of temple.

Twenty rows of candles burned along a veranda set in front of a large red sliding door. Foxes standing on hind legs danced with people in a large relief painted on its surface. Dominic looked down, avoiding eye contact with the statues and jogged up to the foot of the temple. He paused for a moment at the threshold, unsure what to do.

He knocked on the door. "Konnichiwa." It was the worst approximation of a Japanese accent ever. "Sorry to disturb you. I need to use your phone!"

No response. He knocked harder, hoping someone was inside but just didn't quite hear him. Nothing stirred. Dominic found himself pounding on the door in desperation. *Someone surely had to be in if candles were burning?*

The door shifted under Dominic's assault and some of the heavy wax paper attached to its frame dented. He pulled it open, frustration overcoming any thoughts of trespass. Inside more candles burned, set along the temple's interior walls. Two large statues glared at Dominic from the opposite side, standing sentinel over a large wooden box in the centre of the room.

He stepped inside, lowering his gaze to avoid the statues' accusing eyes. The temple's interior had no furnishings, no side rooms, only the statues, box and a sliding barrier at the rear. Dominic's hope faded, there was no phone here, only some kind of ancient shrine. The candles had probably been lit by a warden during the day, left to burn down overnight.

"What do I do now?" Dominic cupped his head in his hands. Returning down the path might lead to a road or a village. There was nothing here that could help. At least following the other route provided a little hope of rescue.

Dominic turned and walked towards the door.

"Aren't you going to present an offering?"

Dominic whipped round, heart pounding. The sliding door at the rear of the temple had moved and a young girl sat swinging her legs on the wooden box. She looked like a teenager, Japanese, but with bright orange hair. She wore loose red pants and a white top bound by a sash. Her headband had small fox like ears sticking out of it.

"An offering?" He cursed himself for missing the more obvious question. "You speak English?"

"That's a stupid question." The girl frowned. "I'm speaking it right now."

Her eyes reflected the firelight making it difficult to tell their colour, but they reminded Dominic of the statues. She stared at him, a grin playing across thin lips.

"So, are you going to leave an offering or not?" She gestured to the box.

Dominic pulled his wallet out. He had a few dollars in there along with some ten thousand Yen notes. It was a lot to give away but Dominic found himself pulling out one of the notes, walking towards the girl, and then placing it through a small gap in the box.

Did I do that right? Dominic wasn't sure, but from the approving nod his actions earned him, he must have followed the correct etiquette. She hopped off the box and leaned down to peer at Dominic from an odd angle. The girl cocked her head like a dog regarding a treat, then smiled.

She smelled strongly of jasmine and the sweet smell reminded Dominic of his grandmother's house. She always burned jasmine scented candles, claiming they kept the bad spirits away.

"What's your name?" The girl stood behind Dominic now, tip toeing to peer over his shoulder.

"I'm Dominic." He looked up to find the girl now standing in front of him again. "And you?"

"Kitsune."

"That's a strange name." Dominic wasn't even sure how to pronounce it. "Is it foreign?" he kicked himself mentally the instant the words left his mouth.

Kitsune glared at him. "You're strange!"

She hopped back onto the offertory box. It seemed disrespectful to do so, but scolding her seemed pointless. She stood, legs spaced apart, staring down at him.

"Can you help me?" Dominic pointed to the back of the temple, "Do you have a phone I can use? I'm lost in the woods and need to get back to my hotel."

"There's no phone here."

Dominic waited, but Kitsune said nothing else. She just stood there staring at him. It was possible she was crazy, but given how isolated he felt even a crazy person had to be better than nothing.

"So…"

Kitsune sighed, hopping off of the box again. "Fine, I'll take you to what you seek."

Relief washed over Dominic. He was finally going to escape this nightmare, get back to a warm bed and be back with Anna in his comfortable hotel room. He could deal with any problems tomorrow, now he just wanted to get back.

Kitsune brushed her hand gently across Dominic's. A warm sensation ran up his arm and into his head. The sensation brought back more memories. The feel of Anna's hand in his, her soft skin against his own. Sunlight beamed down on them from above, they were having a conversation about a special trip.

The images changed. He was in a car, but he wasn't driving. He sat on the backseat, someone next to him. Their hands locked together, the feeling warm and comforting. Someone in the front of the car was laughing. He had his mobile in his other hand, it felt important to hang onto it.

He couldn't remember the other person's face, was it Anna's?

The memory faded before he could recall their face, leaving only the feel of their touch and a growing sense of disorientation. His skin tingled where Kitsune had touched it. The hair band she wore was very well made. He couldn't make out any joins or seams. It made the fox like ears blend in perfectly with her hair.

She paused at the temple entrance. "Come, time to go home."

Kitsune walked annoyingly slow. Every pace she took was measured. Dominic bumped into her as she paused and looked around.

"Sorry…" Dominic felt something soft and furry against his leg. It withdrew quickly, probably some kind of animal. "Sorry for bumping into you. But can we walk any faster?"

"No."

"Can I ask why?"

"No."

"Look," Dominic walked ahead of his companion and turned to face her. "I appreciate the help, but I need to get back to my hotel, people must be worried about me."

Kitsune cocked her head, such a bizarre habit. She stood staring without saying a word. Dominic was about to give up, thank her and go off on his way when she put her hand on his shoulder. The same warm feeling at her caress flooded through his body.

"There's no rush." She smiled and removed her comforting touch. "They will wait for you, I'm certain of it."

"How long until we find a phone or village?"

"Soon."

"How soon?"

"How long does it take to walk down a street?" Kitsune gestured down the paved pathway.

"Uh…" Dominic wasn't sure what the girl meant by that, what street? The street where he grew up? The Ware Road; it was a long road in a small commuter town outside London, not something a person could walk down quickly.

"Ten minutes?"

"That's how long it'll take." Kitsune resumed her measured paces. Thankfully she moved slightly quicker now, but still slow enough to make Dominic wish he had picked a faster guide.

Dominic checked his phone as they walked but the screen flickered, still frozen at the moment it broke. It was strange how the battery had kept going despite the constantly lit screen. His watch wasn't much help either, still fixed at 9:15pm.

"So." A little conversation might help the time pass.

"Do you work at that temple?"

"You could say that." Kitsune didn't bother turning round to reply.

"Where do you live?"

"At the temple."

"How old are you? Where are your parents?"

"Old?" Kitsune stopped. "Not that old. My parents live around the temple too." The pacing resumed after her pause for thought.

"Are they out right now?"

"You could say that." Kitsune turned on her feet and grinned.

"That's a cute headband." Dominic sought for anything to keep the conversation going, unnerved by the girl's constant smiling.

"Headband? I'm not wearing one."

Dominic wanted to interject as Kitsune stopped again. She stared at him robbing Dominic of all questions. Her eyes had taken on a golden glow under the moonlight. Her stare made Dominic want to avert his gaze, but he was transfixed. No matter how hard he tried, he couldn't look away.

"Did you love Anna?"

"What?" Dominic wasn't sure how to respond. The question brought Dominic up short. He stopped staring at the ground as he fought to remember. The pillow fight at the hotel. Anna smacking a pillow across the side of his head when he wasn't looking, then falling to the floor pretending to be hurt when he retaliated.

They did the same thing at home. They watched movies together with bags of chocolate buttons, they held hands looking up at the stars. The memories came but the feelings wouldn't.

"I…I think so."

"Why are you crying?"

Dominic reached up to feel a line of wetness across his cheek. Why was he crying? Anna was safe back at the hotel waiting for him, all he had to do is find a phone and everything would be okay, wouldn't it?

"I think you loved her dearly," Kitsune whispered.

Dominic nodded; if he was crying he must have. The whole situation made his head feel fuzzy, a cloud of fog refusing to lift from the life he used to lead. The only thing he had left to hold onto was the strange girl who was leading him to God knows where.

"Come. We still have a way to walk."

"I thought you said it was only ten minutes away?"

"It is."

Kitsune no longer paced ahead, she walked alongside him, stepping carefully but no longer at an annoyingly slow pace. Even his watch showed progress; five minutes had now passed since he last checked. It wasn't broken after all.

Ahead the trees began thinning. Dominic could even see the distant glow of streetlights through the dense trunks.

A faint smell of exhaust smoke wafted in the cold air.

"Almost there, Dominic." Kitsune picked up her pace. She walked faster now. She hunched over, her face thrust forward.

"I thought there wasn't any rush?"

"There wasn't."

Kitsune broke out into a run. Stooped over like an athlete at the end of a sprint. Dominic struggled to keep pace. He didn't feel breathless, just tired, like something was pulling him back. He managed a glance at his watch, nine minutes had now passed.

"*Almost time.*" Kitsune's voice distorted, taking on a disembodied quality.

Kitsune was on all fours now, loping down the paved path. Something long and furry burst from underneath her trousers, Dominic stared as twin white tipped orange tails swished around violently as they pelted along the pathway.

"What the Hell?"

"*There's no Hell here. Keep running or we'll be too late,*" she growled in reply.

There was a road ahead. Dominic could see traces of blue light flashing and the smell of smoke was more pungent now. He could even hear voices up ahead. He couldn't understand them, they must have been speaking Japanese. Finally, it was time to go home.

Kitsune's clothing fell away, her entire body covered in fur. Her face had distended, taking on a vulpine aspect. Her form had shrunk to half its size as they ran. Dominic was too relieved to care. Maybe it was a hallucination? It didn't matter, he was almost there.

Dominic burst from the forest path into the road, with Kitsune close beside him. His breath caught in his throat. His entire world crumbled in a second as he stood dumbfounded at the scene unfolding before him.

59

Police cars surrounded a crashed blue mini. A dark-haired woman stood with a policewoman wrapping a blanket around her; she was crying. *Anna?* An ambulance was parked close by with paramedics working on someone. He could see the person's face. Blue lips, blood soaking one side. Green eyes staring vacantly up at the sky. Cold reality set in as Dominic recognised himself.

His vision blurred as memories resurfaced all at once. They had been given a ride by a friend of the hotel owners. They didn't have much money so they accepted it without question, after all they could trust him.

They were on the way to visit a shrine, and a fox had run out into the road. The driver swerved to avoid it and the car had crashed. The text had come in just before the accident. Dominic was looking at his phone when it happened.

"Do you remember now?" Kitsune asked.

"Yes…" The Dominic on the road wasn't breathing, and the paramedics and police officers were checking their watches. Ten minutes had passed.

"Was that you on the road?" Dominic had so many questions, but the only one that came to mind was that.

"No. That was a silly little creature that shouldn't have been running across roads. She escaped. You didn't. So I came."

"What happens to me now?" A single tear rolled down Dominic's cheek as he turned to look at Anna. Anna screamed, pounding her fists against a police officer. She tried to run over to his body but the policewoman held her back.

"Now? Now you come with me. This isn't your place anymore."

"I don't want to go."

"Nobody does." Kitsune rubbed her cheek on Dominic's

leg. *"But this is Hitzusen; Inevitability in your language. It was meant to be. You belong with me now."*

Dominic stood, staring at Anna as a dull ache settled in his chest. He wanted to run over to her, comfort her. This could all be a dream, an hallucination brought about by the accident. He could wake up in bed next to her. The idea was comforting.

"One day the dream has to end," Kitsune whispered.

Dominic shivered, his body feeling leaden as he tried to walk towards Anna. A voice whispered into his ear but he couldn't tell where it came from. No matter how hard he tried to focus, its words eluded him. Kitsune gently tapped him on the shoulder, bringing Dominic back to the moment, the voice fading.

She stood beside him, back in her human form. She reached out and gently took his hand. A warm feeling flowed through his entire body. He felt himself rising, being lifted as light surrounded him. Dominic felt nothing but warmth all around him as he shut his eyes and floated into inevitability.

About the author
David Trebus is an enthusiastic Creative Writing MA student and budding PhD candidate from Hertfordshire. He has always been inspired by mythology, folk lore and all things supernatural. He currently has several published works including a novel, short stories and a comic.

Kitsune is the first in a series of interlocking short stories based around Dominic and his girlfriend Anna's experiences with the supernatural.

Following the Thread

Margaret Bulleyment

"I remember this last one – The Weston Barton cope, early fourteenth century – from the exhibition poster." Adam peered down at the faded embroidery. "It's the angel playing the lute, riding the spotty horse with the ridiculous expression on its face. That horse is definitely not a music lover, Gran. Hang on, while I get you nearer. This wheelchair's an absolute…"

"Aargh, that's my foot." Someone whacked heavily into Adam's shoulder.

"Sorry, sorry. Are you all right?" he mumbled, through a mouthful of curls.

"I'll count my toes and let you know," said the girl, regaining her balance.

"I do apologise. My grandmother has a super electric wheelchair, but we had to swap it for this museum monstrosity to get into the exhibition." Adam paused, looking at his victim. He had never been so close to anyone with blue hair before and even the dim museum light could not tone down the colour. "Usually, the opposite sex do not hurl themselves at me – more's the pity."

"It's my fault," Eva broke in. "Wheelchairs aren't suitable in here, but I really wanted to see this exhibition. How often do you get to see craftsmanship like this? How did they manage seven hundred years ago, to sew so exquisitely in dark little workshops without electric light?" She waved her magnifying glass. "I just wish I could see more of it."

"This cope is the very best exhibit." The girl moved forward and brushing Adam aside, swung the wheelchair round and gently guided Eva's arm and the magnifying glass, upwards. "Look up here, at the beautiful split-stitching on the morse – the Lamb of God in gold and silver thread – all raised in relief. Dazzling! It's such a pity, you can't touch it. Textiles are made to be touched."

"You're so right," agreed Eva.

"I thought Morse was a detective," muttered Adam.

"It's the clasp that holds the cope on the priest's chest," the girl explained. "It's the most ornate piece of the cope. It's separated here, because they cut the cope up at some point and it became an altar covering."

"How long have you worked here?" asked Eva.

"I haven't. I've just finished art college. Textiles. But I did live in Weston Barton, when I was a child. Meet my village treasure, found in a battered church chest in Victorian times. It's been on permanent loan to this museum for over a century. Usually only the morse is on display here, but every twenty years or so the whole cope travels from London to the village church for a couple of days, escorted by security guards."

"That's where I first saw it when I was a small child. I'd literally never seen anything like it. I was absolutely fascinated – especially with all the martyrs scattered in the corners, suffering gory deaths. I even remember Mum and I bringing a lemon cake for the security guards."

"People steal embroidery?" Adam laughed.

"Forgive my grandson's ignorance," said Eva. "He studied mathematics. Now, I suggest that to make up for your bruised toes and to thank you for your expertise, all three of us have lunch together. I'm Eva and this is Adam, the Toe-Crusher."

"Thank you. That's really kind of you. I'm Izzy."

"Let's go." Adam grabbed the wheelchair back and steered it firmly out of the gloomy exhibition room into the light of the lobby. Transferred back into her own chair, Eva was in control again and once out of the museum, was careering along the pavement, talking animatedly with Izzy.

Adam was relegated to bringing up the rear. In the sunlight, Izzy's curls looked bluer than ever and with the many layers she was wearing under a white, fluffy jacket, trailing behind her, Adam thought she looked like a circus tent on a windy day – a very irritating tent.

"This is one of our favourite brasseries, Izzy," said Eva, turning off the pavement as the door slid open in front of her. "Table for three, Jean."

"I only usually have a sandwich, Eva, so…"

"My treat, Izzy. Have what you like. Some proper French onion soup with a salad, perhaps? I always have confit of duck, and Adam has steak, so you're the only one who needs to order."

"That would be great. Thanks."

The wine appeared on cue, as they reached the table.

"To new friends!" toasted Eva. "So you're a textiles student? What are you planning now you've finished college?"

"I'm not sure. It's complicated." Izzy fiddled with a piece of bread. "My Mum died two years ago and my dad a year later, so the cottage in Weston Barton is now mine, but I'm still sharing a flat here in London. Do I stay up here, or move to Oxfordshire? If I knew what I was doing next, it would make the choice much easier."

The conversation was briefly interrupted as Jean slid the food on to the table.

"I'm so sorry, Izzy," said Eva. "You're very young to lose both your parents."

"They were quite old when I was born and after Mum died, Dad just faded away. The problem is all this happened when I should have been planning my first career steps and now I've lost the thread completely. I can't do anything until I've sorted out the cottage and it's a real mess."

"Young people now, have so many more choices and opportunities than previous generations, but they seem to have more problems dealing with them." Eva looked pointedly at Adam.

"Gran is saying that in spite of three glorious – sometimes, mathematical – years at uni, I'm not sure of my next step either. Gran was a teacher. You know where you are with that."

"Until sewing and textiles became Fabric Technology," said Eva. "Then I became a tutor at *The Royal School of Needlework*, but now my eyesight means I can no longer do any of those things."

Izzy put down her spoon. "You must be a wonderful needlewoman."

"No, that was my mother. She embroidered for Norman Hartnell."

"Wow! I'm impressed. Hartnell made the Queen's wedding dress, didn't he? Although I bet your mum didn't end up with a wardrobe of exquisite dresses."

"You're right. Most of the time she only saw panels, or pieces, although she did keep a few odds and ends. Would you like to see them?"

"I'd love to."

"Well, depending on what you're doing this afternoon, you're welcome to come back home with me now and look at them. I don't live very far away."

"That would be great.'

"But before that, let's have a dessert. The chocolate mousse is why I come here."

"Shame, they've never learned how to make proper bread and butter pudding," said Adam. "I think I've had enough needlework for today. All I know about Norman

Hartnell is that he was the first Dr Who's, second cousin. I'll go and order a taxi for us all – unless the Tardis happens to be passing by."

"I love my grandson," whispered Eva to Adam's departing back. "He does so much for me, but I do wish he'd organise himself as well as he organises other people."

"I'm the last person to comment on that," said Izzy.

Eva's apartment was light, colourful and uncluttered. Izzy flew around it. "This wall hanging's fantastic, Eva. What a beautiful blue. Castles in the air, perhaps? A Scandinavian wood?"

"Right on both counts. I've a Swedish friend who's an interior designer and when your sight is failing, you value light and colour above everything. Adam, please fetch Matka's boxes, while I make some tea."

"Do you really want to drag those out again, Gran. Won't it make you…?"

"Please get them, Adam."

By the time Adam had plonked the boxes down unceremoniously on the kitchen table, Eva and Izzy were drinking tea, deep in discussion on the merits of English medieval embroidery over Flemish.

Adam sat down reluctantly, as Eva pushed a cup of tea towards him.

"Now then Izzy, these will interest you," she said, pulling open the nearest box and delving into layers of tissue paper. "These are just sample pieces. Turquoise silk with white embroidery; turquoise on turquoise; white on white. Matka specialised in white on white, but then she had perfect eyesight."

"I'm speechless, Eva – the workmanship. Did your mother ever know where her embroidery ended up? It must be a shame when you've put so much effort into something, to only have a sample – not the whole garment – and then never see your beautiful work again."

"But sometimes the whole world sees it." Eva reached into a second box and unwrapped a silken panel seeded with tiny pearls and beads. "There are pictures of Eva Peron wearing a dress embroidered with the final version of this panel."

"Oh my God! Just look at those exotic entwined flowers. Can I touch it?"

"You can. The flowers are South American ones, of course. And we've also got…" Eva reached into the box again, "…velvet swatches. The royal blue was worn by Princess Margaret, over a cornflower blue embroidered dress. Feel the pile on those."

"The jewel colours are so rich."

Eva turned back to the first box. "Now, further down in here, it's more mundane – scraps and bits – and there's no exquisite embroidery on this one," she laughed, waving a tattered khaki sleeve at Izzy.

"An army jacket?"

"In the Second World War, even Hartnell had to support the war effort. Embroiderers had to man the machines, like anyone else."

"How soulless, when you're used to creating beautiful garments. I'd have hated it."

"Funnily enough, Matka never thought of it like that. Let me show you."

Eva delved down to the bottom of the box. "What do you think these are?" she said holding out her hand to Izzy.

"Six very battered little gold stars?"

Adam snorted into his tea.

Eva reached into the box again. "And this?"

"A very old book that's been read an awful lot, written in a language I can't even guess at."

"It's a book of Greek myths, in Czech," said Eva. "It was my mother's favourite childhood book. Both my parents were Czech. My father, Karel, owned a company founded by his grandfather, Joseph, who'd been apprenticed to a master craftsman in Vienna. Joseph started his own family business making ecclesiastical garments like your cope; dress uniforms; brides' trousseaux. When my mother worked for the business, Karel was already in charge and just before the war, they got married.

"These little stars are all that is left of my mother's larger Magdan David – shield of David, star of David. My parents had to wear one during the war to identify themselves…"

"As… Jews? I understand, Eva."

"When Matka was embroidering, she would always try and initial her work somewhere – hidden away in a hem, or along a seam – so whatever she was making and wherever it ended up, it still had a little bit of her in it.

"In Bohemia during the war, she 'initialled' with a star. Just twelve little stitches made a six-pointed star that said a part of her life was in that garment.

"They had to make uniforms – Nazi ones, with all sorts of elaborate nonsense all over them. Every garment had to be checked, but there was still the odd opportunity to 'lose' a pin, or even better, a thin needle, somewhere that would be painful before it was found. Matka's star would never be found, but it would always be there.

"When Matka was pregnant with me, my father wanted her to leave and head for London where he had some contacts through the business. She refused to go, but Father insisted and eventually with help from his friends, she did. Father said he would send for her when the war was over and embroiderers were favoured above machinists again.

"I was born after Matka's long journey to England and

68

soon she was sewing more uniforms. I was three, when the news came that my father had been shot for hiding other Jews in the factory."

"Oh, Eva…"

"I'll wash up," interrupted Adam grabbing the tea tray, "and don't forget the hairdresser's coming in an hour, Gran."

"I haven't forgotten. It's my eyes that are fading, not my memory," said Eva sharply. "Enough about me. Now Izzy, tell me more about what you've been doing."

"Well… er… my final exhibition was a series of wall hangings," said Izzy quickly. She dumped her bag on the table and began rummaging around. "Somewhere in here, is the exhibition programme. See." She waved a dog-eared piece of paper at Eva. "The centrepiece was a fabric collage that was inspired by my parents' garden in Weston Barton."

Eva peered closely at it. "Very interesting, but a photo probably doesn't do it justice?"

"You have to see it really – the 3D effect, the layers, the colours. I used all sorts of textures, fabrics and some natural objects from the garden, woven in."

"Why not just enjoy the real garden?" said Adam. "Appreciate the 'natural objects' where they are, rather than stuck on a canvas inside."

"Because what's on the canvas is my memories of the garden, as it was, when my parents were alive. It's not the real one. That's a wilderness at the moment."

"Perhaps Adam could look at it for you," suggested Eva. "He worked in a garden centre when he was still at school."

Izzy stood up abruptly. "Thanks. I must be going. I've taken up enough of your time."

"Do come again, Izzy, and if we can help you in any way, do let us know. My son, Adam's dad, is a solicitor, should you need any legal help with your parents' estate."

"Thanks, but all that's done. Now I have to concentrate on what I'm going to do with the cottage. I'm heading up there this weekend. I want to make it habitable. Perhaps I could rent it as a holiday cottage, or something. At present, it's where I store my wall hangings. I've been taking them down there one by one, on the train. Sometimes, I wish I made jewellery."

Eva pulled open the table drawer and handed Izzy a card. "Here are my details. Do keep in touch. You can't imagine how wonderful it's been talking to a fellow enthusiast, Izzy. Adam will show you out."

As Adam stepped into the lift behind her, Izzy turned on him. "Did you have to laugh quite so loudly, when I put my foot in it about the stars?"

"She wanted you to do that. Look, I know you mean well, but my grandmother's not the strong woman she appears – especially to someone who has only just met her. She's accepted her lack of mobility, but her eyesight's another matter. She's got a ninety per cent chance of going completely blind and that wouldn't be easy for anyone, but for someone with her abilities, it'll be dreadful. And all this raking over the past is unhealthy."

"Well, I thought she looked proud of her family and what they'd achieved in difficult circumstances. I find her fascinating. You can't know how good it is to talk to someone who's as passionate about the same things that you are. I wish she'd been my tutor. You're not passionate about anything – except criticising my work because you once worked in a garden centre."

"I've done more than that. I've designed a few gardens. I started with an urban one for Dad and then some of his friends wanted something similar. Maths comes in handy when your ideas have to fit limited spaces."

"Well, any ideas for larger rural spaces are welcome," said Izzy, taking out her phone, as the lift reached the ground floor. Had she really just said that?

"Give me your phone," said Adam, as they stepped through the entrance door. "Perhaps it might be better if we co-ordinated our support for Eva." He took Izzy's phone from her and entered his number. "Call me, if you get any good ideas."

"Will do, if it's only so we can avoid each other," Izzy shouted, sailing off in the direction of the bus stop.

Two weeks later, Izzy was back drinking tea at Eva's kitchen table, which was once again decorated with Matka's boxes. "Could I ask a favour, Eva?"

"Of course, Izzy."

"Are there any little scraps and bits at the bottom of the 'mundane' boxes that I could have for my work?"

"Yes. There's plenty of stuff you can have. I'd much rather it was useful, than just mouldering in the box. Help yourself."

"I'm planning some new wall hangings. Oxfordshire has a big *Artweeks* festival every summer, when artists open their homes and studios to the public. I thought I might show my work, while it's down at the cottage anyway. An old builder friend of Dad's is coming in next week, to start some renovations."

The car scrunched to a halt on the gravel. "Welcome to Weston Barton, home of the famous cope and *Spring Cottage Studios*," announced Izzy, opening the car door and diving in to hug Eva. Adam climbed out of the driver's seat and headed for the boot. He missed Izzy's blue curls, but her long sunny-coloured sundress suited her a lot better than her wintry layers.

He helped Eva into her chair.

"What a delightful spot this is," announced Eva. "Just smell those roses. This beautiful garden's hardly the mess you described, Izzy."

"That's because I've had help," said Izzy, smiling at Adam.

"You don't mean?" Eva turned to Adam.

"Yes, me. Guilty as charged," Adam admitted.

"But you've not mentioned Izzy since we all met six months ago," said Eva.

"Yup. Fooled you, Gran. But just look at what can be achieved when two people stitch a project together."

"Come inside, Eva. I've something I want to show you," said Izzy.

She lead Eva through the front door and dramatically flung open the next door in the hall. "This room is now my studio, as you can see, but for *Artweeks,* I'll be spreading my work all around the ground floor of the cottage, so it makes a sequence people can follow."

"The light in here's brilliant," said Eva, following her in.

"Fortunately, the cottage isn't as old as it looks, so Dad's friend was able to put in full-length windows.

Now this is my new work, Eva. Take a good look."

"The colours are wonderful, but I just need my magnifying glass to look at the details."

"Don't worry about that. Get nearer the canvas, close your eyes and give me your hands.

"Yes," said Eva. "What...?"

"Just follow it," said Izzy. "And can you feel this section, in relief?"

"It feels like a large 'V'."

"Adam told me more about your family and of course, that's the logo of your father's company. Now follow the

72

thread and up here, you can feel a different texture. That's the river Thames, when your mother reached London – it's a little bit of her blue silk. In fact, the whole work is the scraps and bits that have made up your family's life.

That's a little fragment, Adam found from your time at the *RSN*. And here, here and here. Can you feel them? E-V-A. Adam told me your mother called you that because it means 'life,' in Hebrew. Oh and down in this bottom corner… feel that."

"Hair?"

"Yes. I've 'signed' it, with a blue curl. Adam insisted. "We'll look at everything in detail after tea. Now, open your eyes and you can see all of it – here's your magnifying glass – but, it makes more sense if you keep your eyes shut and just follow the thread."

Eva opened her eyes. "I can't believe what you've created from the bottom of the box."

"It's not quite finished. Can you see I've embroidered some little gold stars along your lifeline? I just wondered whether you'd let me sew your mother's ones in the same places? When the festival's over next month, we'll be delivering this to you in London, so the stars will be with you all the time."

"That would be a perfect place for them. I can't thank you enough, Izzy. I'm speechless."

"That's not something I ever expected to hear," said Adam. 'Oh and there's more. At the moment the garden is just tidied up for the festival, but I'll be coming down here and re-designing it and I need your help with that. It's going to be a sensory garden, so everyone can enjoy it. The roses and the honeysuckle are a good start, but I have a lot of other ideas."

"Now all this is done, I'm moving in properly and living here," said Izzy. "I've already got some commissions from people seeing your canvas in progress."

73

"And I've decided to make a business from my garden design," said Adam, "for which I also need a rural location. There's a building in the garden that was Izzy's dad's office that will be perfect."

"You know," said Eva, "when my mother was little, she loved the picture of the Three Fates in her Greek myths book. Before she understood they were spinning the threads of everyone's life, she thought they were dressmakers."

"I am humbled to finally know the true place of needlework in my life," laughed Adam.

"And thinking of life's important decisions," said Izzy. "Shall I go blonde for *Artweeks?*"

About the author

Margaret Bulleyment began writing fiction and plays, after a long career in comparative education. She has had short stories published in anthologies, including Bridge House's *Snowflakes* and *Baubles,* in Chapeltown's *CaféLit* and on story websites. Her children's play *Caribbean Calypso* was runner-up in Trinity College of Music and Drama's 2011 International Playwriting Competition, and is available on *TreePress*. She has twice had short plays performed professionally, as a finalist in the *Ovation Theatre Awards*.

Footwork

Mary Bevan

Just his luck – no one here to have a drink with. Alesandro gazed resentfully at the scruffy terrace with its cracked paving stones and bleached-out sun umbrellas. Beyond it, in the distance, lay the beach and a sparkling expanse of sea, mocking him with its invitation to pleasure. A precious day off work, and here he was with a knee so painful that he had hardly been able to hobble as far as this shabby little café-bar.

In any case, he thought bitterly, if he could have made it to the beach he would only have had to pretend to laugh at the men's crude jokes about his borrowed crutch, or, worse still, see the pity and disdain in the eyes of the girls who taunted him with their glistening, brown bodies.

So he had spent the morning in bed, dozing until the heat in the cramped bedroom he shared with the commis-chef – newly-arrived at the Hotel Villarosa but already ridiculously popular with everyone – had become unbearable. Then he had made his way down here, slowly and painfully, to cheer himself up with a few drinks and perhaps some interesting conversation.

It was still relatively early in the season; the barman was watching a football match on a the flickering television screen, and the terrace was empty except for a couple perched on stools at a small counter in the far corner. They were deep in conversation and hardly glanced at him as he limped to a table at a suitable distance from them.

Sipping the first of what he promised himself would be a fair few drinks – after all, what else was there to do – Alesandro studied the couple. The girl, tanned and shapely, was sitting with her back to him, her curtain of black, glossy hair blocking his view of her companion so that most of the time all he could see of him was a pair of long brown arms and slender hands like those of a piano player with which he gestured frequently. His girlfriend, as Alesandro took her to be, was wearing a tight-fitting white sheath with a single stripe of gold, sparkling material meandering from the shoulder line all the way down the dress on one side. There was something mesmerising about the way the sun played on that stripe, emphasising its zig-zag motion so that it seemed like a golden snake with a sinuous life of its own.

As his eyes traced its downward movement, Alesandro noticed something else. Whereas she held the top half of her body still for the most part, her feet seemed in constant motion. First, they would be sitting neatly side by side on the rung of the bar stool in their gold sandals, then first one, then the other, would shake off it shoe, exposing blood-red painted toenails. Next the bare feet would begin to jostle and nudge each other, gently at first, until the mood seemed to change and there would be a kind of hostile collision, after which each foot would search urgently on the ground for its sandal as if to protect itself from attack. He watched fascinated as these rituals were repeated with ever-growing urgency.

Perhaps she felt his stare, for she turned suddenly and fixed her large, dark eyes on him so intently that he was forced to look away in embarrassment. After a suitable length of time he checked that she was no longer looking his way and resumed his fascinated observation. Whether it was the heat, or the effect of alcohol on an empty stomach, he found himself fantasising about those little feet with the blood-red nails – about taking them captive, halting their motion and stroking them into submission. So when she turned round again he was a little bolder, holding her gaze deliberately. Let her see that he fancied her: after all, it lent some interest to an otherwise wasted afternoon. He was startled to find that this time she responded to his look by flicking a lock of hair provocatively off her face before slowly turning away again.

Excited and a little confused – it was a long time since any girl had come on to him like this – he decided to give himself a breathing space by making his way indoors to find the toilet. His head spinning a little from the mixture of pain killers and alcohol, he told himself he would go to the bar and order a sandwich on his way back out, but as he closed the door of the cloakroom behind him he was astonished to find the girl apparently waiting for him a little way up the corridor.

She came quickly to his side, saying in a low, throaty voice, "You work at the Villarosa, don't you? I've seen you there. Quick, you must listen."

Confused, he stammered, "Yes. What…?"

"Please, you will stay here until we go?"

It was an appeal rather than a question so he said quickly, "Yes, if you want me to. I mean, I was going to get a sandwich anyway."

She nodded and flicked her hair from her face again so that he could see the outline of her high cheekbones and slender neck. He saw now that her eyes were deepest brown with gold flecks in them. Oh but she was beautiful!

"Oh thank you, thank you so much. I am very frightened, you see. I don't want to be alone with him. You will stay?"

Not knowing which of many possible questions to ask first, he managed only a shrug of assent. But it was enough. She smiled, eyes narrowing and lips pouting. How he wanted to pull her to him, help himself to handfuls of that glossy hair. Clearly, she read his thoughts for, laying a manicured hand lightly on his arm and giving him a look that could only be read as an invitation, she turned away and was gone.

Alone again, Alesandro leaned against the wall and took a deep breath. The damned crutch! It had stopped him making a pass at her. What did she mean? Why was she afraid? But she had noticed him at the hotel. And the way she had looked at him! Closing his eyes, he saw himself with her at the beach, introducing her to the others, an arm thrown carelessly round her shoulders as she leaned her head against him. They would not be so quick to dismiss him then! But what was he thinking of? He must get back outside: she would expect it. He pulled himself together and limped out, picking up an extravagant vodka and lime at the bar on his way.

On the terrace, all was just as it had been before. The girl and her partner were still deep in conversation, though now the man seemed more agitated and spoke more loudly so that Alesandro was able to catch the words 'listen', and 'impossible'. His girl's feet (for he now thought of her as *his* girl), circled and fought each other ever more furiously.

In his hurry to get back outside he had forgotten to order his sandwich and realised he was feeling distinctly light-headed, but what did it matter? What should he do next? How to get in touch with her? Would she leave a message at his hotel?

He was so absorbed in these thoughts that at first he was hardly aware of the raised voices in the inner bar, but now the noise increased, and looking up he saw a group of young people spilling out on to the terrace, laughing and talking. Damn. The invasion threatened to break the spell of the afternoon. Besides, they were blocking his view of the table in the corner. Pulling himself to his feet he had begun to thread his way carefully around the edge of the terrace, skirting the groups of newcomers, when he felt someone tap his shoulder. He turned to see who it was and was amazed to find the girl close beside him, breathing heavily, her face flushed. He was shocked to see that the hand she now laid on his arm was glistening with fresh blood. What had the beast done to her? He would kill him for this! He began to frame a question but she shook her head to stop him, grasped his hand and pressed something sticky into it. Then in a flash she was gone. He saw the sparkling stripe on her dress snake its way to the back of the terrace and disappear over the low wall that enclosed it.

Only when he could no longer see her did he think to look down at what she had given him. To his amazement he saw that he was holding a knife that was dripping blood down his trousers and over his shoes. Confused, he stood there, just as she had left him, staring down at it.

Somewhere he heard a woman cry out, "An ambulance, get an ambulance – he's bleeding to death!"

"No," he blurted out, "I'm alright. It's nothing. There's been some mistake," but then he realised no one was looking at him. All their attention was focussed on the table in the far corner, where a young man lay slumped in a widening pool of blood.

But someone had heard his protests: a young girl turned towards him, pointed and screamed, "Look, he's over here, the murderer! He's got a knife, look!"

Time seemed to slow as he saw two men detach themselves from the group and begin to move towards him, menacingly. On the periphery of his vision he thought he saw a band of gold glittering far off in the distance – but then perhaps it was just the sun in his eyes.

About the author
Mary is a former lecturer who is having a great time using retirement to write as she always promised herself she would. Concentrating on flash fiction and short stories, she has won prizes in competitions including Flash 500, Tethered by Letters and Writers' Bureau, and has been published in *Momaya Review*, *Best of Café Lit*, *South*, *This Little World*: *Anthology of Dorset Writers* and *1000 Words of Less* (Australia).

Magpie

Sally Angell

When the new shopfront in town was revealed, Ellie was drawn to the window. Anything to lift the grey cloak of her day.

She peered up at the sign, and was dazzled by swirly pink and purple letters that spelt out the name: *Magpie.* The hopefulness of it made her throat ache. Here, on this dingy street, where retailers were giving up and closing each week, someone had created an oasis of sparkle and colour. Ellie did a quick assessment of the entrance, but knew she had to go inside.

A man in a black overall darted forward, as Ellie scraped the wheels through the doorway. He pushed the wheelchair over to a corner for her, positioning it to face a row of lamps that glowed with soft light.

Ellie snapped the chair brake on, and took off the waterproof cover. "You stay there, Hero," she instructed. As if he could go anywhere else! But it always made her feel better to talk to him.

"He's got beautiful eyes," the shop man smiled.

People always said that. And they were indeed; large and soft and a lovely deep brown. But useless. Not that Hero was blind. His vision was quite good. It was just that what he saw didn't mean anything to him.

"Your...?"

"Son," Ellie clarified. Sometimes strangers thought she was one of those support workers who supervised clients on trips to the town centre, helping them do shopping tasks. If clocking that Ellie was actually the mother of the thirty-ish man she was pushing around, their faces changed. Pity usually. It made Ellie annoyed. She'd had joy and grief, like any other parent. But it was her life and that was that. It could be hard though. Especially now.

She'd stuffed the envelope from the council offices in her pocket before she came out. There was always something, some minefield of bureaucracy to cope with. It was time for a Review, the letter stated, giving the appointment date for a re-assessment of Mr Hero Smith's needs. Ellie winced as pain shot through her ankle.

"This isn't a charity shop," the man explained. Although one did like to stock general knick-knacks from house clearances and donations. But he knew about the stuff that was worth more, he said, from the dealers. So sometimes a vase from the nineteen-fifties, say, would cost that bit more because it was a particular brand. And collectors' items were obviously going to be pricier.

Ellie nodded, trying to blot the worries from her mind. How would she take Hero for his assessment if her foot got worse? And then there was the shock of spotting Tony walking down the road earlier. Ellie wasn't quite sure if it was him. But still.

To throw off the dark shadows, she turned to the glittering array of goods for sale: jewellery, teapots, pictures, ceramic bowls. All sorts. What a feast. It was lovely in here; none of the grubbiness and smells that lingered even in the best second-hand places that had taken over the high street. As her eyes swept round the room, every surface was clean and shining.

Anticipation shivered through Ellie at the possibility of finding that something special that would be just right for her living room. She picked up a blue glass pot. If she set it on the windowsill the light would shine through it, giving the room a sapphire aura. She'd put loose change by each week and perhaps the shopkeeper would keep it for her until she had enough. That's if the authorities didn't cut her money after the assessment. By spending carefully she could sometimes squeeze the odd treat at the moment, like taking Hero to Greggs' cafe for coffee and a cake. But if their income was cut, even those few everyday pleasures that broke up the day into bearable parts, would stop. She put the glass pot back on the shelf.

More customers were arriving. They seemed like magpies themselves, twittering, eager and curious, sharply ready to swoop in on anything of brilliance in their line of vision.

"Mm m – m – m – mm – m – mmm." Hero was getting fretful. He wasn't good with crowds. Ellie sighed. Time to go.

The shop man – 'Call me John' – held the door open, as Ellie manoeuvred the chair out onto the grimy pavement. "See you again." His pupils were sharp and piercing in the afternoon gloom, but in a kind way.

It was two days before Ellie went back. She daren't answer the front door at home in case it was Tony. And the need for a doctor's appointment for her foot was getting urgent. She phoned at eight in the morning as they said but the line was engaged. And when she got through the second day and told them she'd have to bring Hero with her to the clinic, they said no, it's against the rules.

By the third day Ellie had to get out of the house, even if walking was difficult. She kept the image of the treasure-filled shop in her mind as she struggled to the bus stop with Hero.

As she flicked through the 'Vintage Range' clothes, hung on a silver rail, Ellie found herself telling confiding in John how Hero used to go to a class. Not that he learnt anything. But the tutor did sensory therapy sessions. She brought in cotton wool with dabs of lavender for the group to sniff, teaspoons of jam to taste, and music CDs to listen to. The teaching assistant held a crayon in Hero's good hand, and drew with it. He brought his piece home. Hero's Artwork. But it was different now. The funding was axed.

"Sometimes," Ellie looked away, "I don't want to wake up in the morning." John made sympathetic noises. "But then, he is the *reason* for me getting out of bed each day."

Ellie popped out, or rather hobbled out, to the newsagent to pay her gas. Back in the warm cocoon of the shop, John made her a mug of peppermint tea, and pulled up a chair. Ellie leaned back, sipping the hot sweet drink. It made her feel sleepy, floating in a wonderland Through the whooziness, she was aware of talking over in the corner where Hero sat. A couple of customers were browsing, but didn't seem to notice.

A few years ago members of the public were told to speak directly to adults with learning difficulties, now the blanket term for any disability. TV adverts urged the public to speak *to* them, not about them as if they weren't there. A lot of people found that difficult and felt self-conscious.

But John was chatting away to Hero quite naturally. "Shall I put this here, do you think? No, you're right. It would look better next to the copper kettle." It made Hero calmer. Ellie could sense it. His breathing was easier, and the humming dropped to a murmur of content.

And Ellie too was relaxed and at ease. John left Hero to snooze and picked up a duster. He handled everything in the shop with love and care, and Ellie closed her eyes and wondered about the life of The Collector, as she called him. Everyone needed something, someone, to keep them going, to give meaning to their days.

She, Ellie, loved Hero, and wouldn't be without him. But sometimes she longed for some response. Not a thank you. That would be unrealistic. And a bond was too much to hope for. A connection?

That's what having kids is like, friends sighed, when she this admitted this yearning. "You give and give," they said, "and then give some more. And for sod all."

It made Ellie squirm with irritation. No! Her situation wasn't the same. Children, *normally,* grew up eventually and became independent. They related to you, and helped out as parents got older.

This was Ellie's greatest fear, that she would grow older and not be able to look after Hero. It was twenty-four seven. Getting him up and dressed; the washing; feeding him, changing him, putting him to bed.

Ellie opened her eyes. Hero had fallen asleep. She went over and propped his head up, so he wouldn't have neckache when he woke.

"I'll buy the glass pot next time," Ellie told John, and he said he would put it by. "It's the Review tomorrow." She drew her finger across her throat.

"You are saving the government thousands, by looking after Hero yourself, Ellie." John's usually mild voice became indignant. "You need help. Tell them."

That night, Ellie's dreams were like scenes in a horror movie.

"Yes." An official's disembodied voice. "Your son can walk five steps and move three fingers. He's now fit for work."

If sometimes there was some movement, perhaps a slight turn of the head, or a hand lifting, even a difference in his features, Ellie pretended it hadn't happened. Any reported change would make everything more difficult.

It was mostly forms, when she got there. All through the Review Ellie kept thinking "Is this a trick question?" They didn't seem interested in examining Hero. When she asked about his assessment, they said there was no medical officer now. You'll hear in a week, the interviewer confirmed. She looked like a schoolgirl and kept giggling at something on her phone. What would she know?

A banging on the door that evening drowned out the television. Ellie crept into the hall and shrank back, seeing the silhouette behind the frosted glass. Tony. The old rage flooded through her at the memory of his irresponsibility, though when he'd left it was easier, in a way, to cope without him. If she followed her routines, she could just about survive.

Feeling shaky, she opened the door a few inches. She opened her mouth to say, "What do you want?" but nothing came out.

Ellie was on the orthopaedic ward in the local hospital for a night. They strapped her foot up. The familiar sickening sensation that she'd left Hero somewhere and couldn't get to him, washed over her and she kept trying to get up.

They wanted her bed, so she was discharged next day, with instructions to keep her foot elevated for twenty four hours. Panic gripped her in the taxi home. How was she going to do that?

"I'll take him out, so you can recover." Tony offered. He had stayed to mind Hero overnight. Ellie fought with herself, as she always did when she needed a rest or an hour's freedom to give her a break but didn't want other people taking her place. Not that she kept Hero isolated. She took him to groups and to see people. But there was always the fear that someone would take him away.

He likes going into that new antique shop on London Road, she told Tony. He'd probably try to leave his son in there, while he put a bet on. The bookie's was just around the corner. But Ellie couldn't be choosy. And she needed time to think.

The council judgement had arrived yesterday. She'd put

off opening it. Later, she'd peeled the flap open, so that the heavy black typing was just visible. She'd put it away in the drawer until she felt strong enough to face what it said.

"As your circumstances have not changed…" Hero's allowance would remain the same! Ellie felt a stone lighter. And the printed words looked friendlier, more of a shimmery grey. There was more.

"Due to your son's difficulties a careworker will be allocated to attend to his needs, getting him up in the morning and at settling him at night." *And* – Ellie went dizzy – "You, as his carer, are entitled to one afternoon each week of respite care, so you have some free time to go out."

The relief made everything look different, as if the world had righted itself. Ellie couldn't see the patches in the kitchen that needed redecorating, just a bright, colourful and cheery place, like *Magpie's* enchanting interior. She could hardly wait to go back there. She would buy a couple of pieces for herself, and a lamp with a coloured bulb for Hero.

When her foot was safe to walk on, Tony said he'd Hero-sit. "I'd like to help sometimes." And Ellie found herself saying yes, he would like that. She got the shuttle bus that very morning, and when she got off walked as quickly as possible to the shop. At first she thought she'd gone the wrong way. But everything else was there.

It was gone. Like so many others along that row, boarded up with white wood or metal sheeting, *Magpie's* façade was no more. Ellie's breath stopped. Vaguely she was aware of other people's knowing comments. A moonlight flit, they said.

When Ellie got home, and after Tony had gone, she just sat there watching the afternoon grow darker. She hadn't the strength to move Hero to the armchair. Eventually he stirred.

As Ellie got up, something twinkled up at her. The wheelchair had a ledge for shopping at the bottom, that Ellie never used because of the bending. She clipped carrier bags over the handle of the chair instead. But a fastener on the cover of the tray had come undone.

Ellie eased herself onto the carpet, reached into the nest of bubble-wrap and saw the shiny stash: a high-carat gold necklace she'd admired in its case, the blue glass trinket; a picture of yellow sunflowers in a frame, a handbag, and a few other bits and pieces that she'd coveted. And something else in a plastic bag.

At first Ellie thought, "Oh no. Tony." Once light-fingered… but then she noticed the scrap of paper.

Ellie's things. Lamp is for Hero.

Ellie stared. She felt like a thief, like someone or some creature who had stolen objects of desire because the temptation was too great. She ought to return them. But where to? And John must want her to have them, or he wouldn't have put the hoard there.

She unwrapped the lamp, and plugged it in.

"MMMM…mmmMM."

In the bright light Hero's eyes had some focus, and it was as if he could see her. Ellie felt the lightest touch, looked down at his hand on her arm, and then covered it with her own.

About the author

Sally Angell loves literature and writing, and is always aiming to develop new and original ideas in her work. Sally explores the truth and reality of feelings, the originality of language and the possibilities of words. She likes to write stories with contemporary themes, that also have a universal meaning. Her writing has been published in magazines and anthologies, and read on radio.

Moe

L.F. Roth

The tiger holds her, its eyes cold, distant. Mesmerized, she blocks the man's way, paying no heed to the rush-hour crowd around them. "Truly amazing." Her words come in a whisper. "So lifelike. So in control." Due to the man's tan, even the colour is right. "Where did you have it done?" With his shirt unbuttoned halfway down his chest, exposing most of the tiger's head, the question doesn't feel intrusive.

"You like it?"

She confirms that she does.

"It was either that or a wolf."

"I'm a cat lover myself. Dogs I can do without."

"So you'd have picked the tiger, too."

She hesitates.

"A cub, perhaps."

His is full-grown; it needs a chest twice the size of hers. Three times. She casts a quick glance at the man's face. He's neither wolf, nor tiger. His hair, unkempt, might turn into a lion's mane if left to grow, but is a little dark. He has a drawn look.

But if he's tired, he isn't the least bashful. There's a pub around the corner, he says. How about they drop in? To her surprise, she accepts. And though they split after one drink, they exchange not only names but phone numbers. Elaine. Gene.

So it goes.

Engrossed in thoughts of the tiger, she arrives home, checks her mail. None. Miriam welcomes her, while Alice and Misha hang back. "Salmon today," she tells them, having stopped at the Co-op on the way home. She takes her shopping into the kitchenette, cleans the cats' tray to get rid of the smell, feeds them.

Eeny, Meeny, Miny, Moe had been their names when there were four of them, but having lost Moe, she renamed the others so as not to be reminded constantly that her favourite was gone. Now, in spite of that, the children's counting rhyme comes to mind – catch a tiger, she thinks. Catch a tiger by the toe. But will Gene's tiger really have toes?

If it does, they'll be down by his knees. She sees them move with each step he takes, as he walks along a sunlit beach, and giggles at the sight.

In the days that follow, she recharges her phone more often than is strictly necessary, but to no avail: he doesn't call. Yet he was the one who'd asked for her number. Of course, he may do that with everyone he meets. He may add names to his contact list just to impress his mates. Come to think of it, he may have got the number wrong. If she doesn't hear from him by Saturday, she could give him a ring. She could, couldn't she?

No. She should wait a full week.

After all, what had they talked about? The tiger, that was it.

The tiger and some friend of his who'd died.

Her own loss had been on the tip of her tongue, but she had kept it to herself. You don't vie for sympathy. But it's hard to know what to say at an unplanned first meeting.

Not anything personal, for sure.

I'm thirty-nine. I have three cats. I'm a receptionist. That would have been quite safe. But would it have defined her?

No more than if she'd stated her real age.

And what would define him? His tiger?

She'll give him a week and after that delete his number.

She goes to work, comes home and feeds the cats. Eventually, the absence of a call is lost among all other absences.

"Chicken today," she tells Miriam, who winds herself around her legs, purring contentedly.

And then, once she has stopped recharging her phone daily, she hears from him – or, to be more precise, he texts her. "Djcu although k civic ncjckvfjdcjv high djfif," she reads. No "hi, hello, how are you"; no signature. Had she deleted him as she'd been of a mind to do, she wouldn't have had a clue who it came from; since she didn't, the display shows his name. She stares at the three proper words; she tries to figure out what the rest could mean. Is this some kind of code? If so, what could "ncjckvfjdcjv" stand for – twelve consonants in a row? Why isn't all of it in code?

Frustrated, she puts the phone down, deciding to ignore it. It could be his idea of a joke.

Unless the text has been jumbled in transit.

She'd better reply. "Hi," she writes. "It seems your tiger got hold of the phone. May I suggest you trim his claws." Having added her name, she presses down on 'send'.

His reply is almost instantaneous. "Just warming up. Letting my fingers dance, to see what might come of it." She has no more than glanced at his message when he is on the phone. Now there's a "hi, how are you" followed by a few bland phrases. Even so, after saying next to nothing, they arrange to meet.

So much for her reserve.

The third time they come together, she learns, to her disappointment, that there are no toes to the tiger; there's no body at all. Lying on her side, she traces the outline of the neck that isn't there, the missing chest and legs, moving down one side and up the other, rounding each of his knees in turn, gliding over the crotch. She also learns that Gene is estranged from his wife.

"Wife," she says. Her hand stops in mid-air. The wife stands over them.

"Estranged," he repeats, as if that was the salient fact. "We don't see eye to eye."

She draws her hand back. "And so you've left her." It's not a question, but the ensuing silence lasts much longer than it should, turning it into one.

She is the one who finally breaks it. "You're saying that you haven't left her."

"I did, for a while. I moved in with a friend. But he died. I told you."

Not as it related to his wife, he hadn't, but no matter. Does he expect her to commiserate?

"I'm a sort of lodger. It simplifies matters."

"Sort of."

"Yes." He turns towards her. "Look, it's a temporary arrangement. It gives me a bed. It provides me with an address. That's all."

Sort of, she thinks; but she doesn't repeat the phrase. Would he have told her if there'd been more to it? An address. A mattress. Given the housing situation, countless people must remain together who would much rather live apart, having fallen out of love.

"Anyway, I never loved her," he points out, as if to correct her thoughts.

And she leaves it at that.

"Make me feel you," he says.

She does.

He's an artist, he informs her.

She had been complaining about the mess at work. The stress. His non sequitur tells her it doesn't interest him. "You paint?" she asks.

"I did some graffiti as a kid. The council had it removed.

But being an artist isn't about what you do. It's a state of mind."

He's sitting on the bed, his feet on the floor, petting Misha. Alice is watching him. So is Miriam, who is keeping an eye on both.

"How?"

"A way of seeing things."

"You mean aesthetically?"

His hand waves away the suggestion and Misha is gone. "Aesthetics have nothing to do with it. It's an awareness of disruptions, of connections. An openness to patterns, patterns that form and disintegrate. To chaos. You know."

Does she? She isn't sure.

"But nothing you do?"

"That will reflect it. But what means you use is immaterial. Paint, you said. Sure. Performance. Film. Photography. Music. Writing."

"Clay," she offers.

"If you want."

Miriam has approached him; she arches her back, rubbing against his leg. Gene puts down his hand and she butts it with her head. Then, without warning, as his thumb strokes her, she bites him. He pulls away with an oath.

Elaine scoops up the cat. "I'm sorry. She's not herself." Holding the cat out of his reach, she inspects the cut. There are a few spots of blood. "You'd better clean it under the tap. I'll get you a plaster." She puts the cat down.

"No need. I'll stay clear of her in future."

"She's probably jealous."

"Well, I won't pet the others either."

Because of me, she'd meant. But she keeps it to herself.

There are no plasters in the bathroom, but she finds one in her handbag. Photography, music, writing, he'd said. "Are you doing anything now?" she asks, returning. "Writing, for example?"

"On and off. I've put down one or two six-word stories lately."

She must have shown her ignorance.

"*He kissed her,*" he says. "*That changed nothing.*"

She remains nonplussed.

"*He kissed him,*" he says. "*That changed everything.*"

She sticks the plaster on his arm, pats it down.

"It started with Hemingway. An American writer."

"William," she declares.

"That was Faulkner. He wrote a story in the form of a sales ad, about a pair of baby shoes that had never been worn. Six words. You're left to figure out why."

"That's sad."

"I used the idea for one of mine. *Closing-down sale. World ends at noon.*"

"The baby shoes are more moving." He flinches; it's not what he wanted to hear. "Of course, it's a bit limited," she adds, making amends. "Are you planning to do a whole book?"

She works out what it would take. With thirty lines to the page, even a slim volume could hold thousands of stories. Who would want to write that many? Who would want to read them?

"You'd probably need illustrations to break it up a bit."

"Stories of one hundred words each would be an alternative. It would be easier. The shorter they are, the greater the challenge."

"I have one," she says. Her fingers mark the rhythm as she counts. "She kept his tiger up all night. Four."

He corrects her. "Seven. And overly optimistic. I have to be on my way." All the same he pulls her down beside him.

They meet at irregular intervals and always, as soon as their initial dates are disposed of, at her place. Mostly this is every few days, but sometimes a week or two will pass between visits. He doesn't stay the night. She wonders why. Once bitten, twice shy, she reckons – and it's his marriage she is thinking of, not Miriam. But they wouldn't have to get married. And if it isn't that, if it's the size of her flat that worries him, as she suspects, it shouldn't be impossible to find a slightly larger place if they really set their hearts on it. One more room would do. It would be one step up from the bed he occupies at his ex-wife's place. Well, ex-wife-to-be, maybe – Elaine still isn't sure they are divorced.

Early on, after he had been away for a while, she let him know she missed him. "Don't count the days," he texted back. "Make the days count."

"Witty," she replied, "but how can I, all on my own?"

He has a store of clichéd phrases, the kind you find set in cheap frames in bric-a-brac shops. "Today's the first day of the rest of your life" is one of them. Hearing it, she'd made a face in response, which had offended him. "What's wrong with it?" he'd said. "It's true, isn't it?"

Yet all his visits occur at the end of the day and present nothing like a new beginning. He doesn't take her out. He's frowned at cinemas, pubs, theatres. Here is where they belong, accompanied by her three cats.

At least, she concludes, he is considerate. He doesn't turn up unannounced. He doesn't let her down. If something intervenes, he texts her, though without stating the reason. It's not that he is secretive exactly, but as if she occupies, as if he would like to see her occupy, a sphere of her own, drifting above whatever else there is. She should be grateful, shouldn't she?

Therefore, she is surprised when, after a few months, he offers something of an excuse. Her phone bleeps and the message reads: "Sorry. Can't get away. Will be in touch."

Can't get away. It must be from home – there's nowhere else for him to get away from, as far as she knows. So what could keep him there? Nothing that she can think of. It won't be his wife, unless their relations are very different from what he has implied. What if there is a child? His wife's? That must be it. No wonder they're estranged; she must have had an affair and got pregnant. But would he babysit someone else's child? It sounds unlikely. Perhaps it's not his wife's. Perhaps some friend of his had no one to turn to at short notice and left his child with him. Just for an hour or two. Would he? Please? She can't imagine him doing it professionally. Well, maybe. The one time she'd approached him about work, he had implied he takes what comes his way, on a short-term basis, to remain as free as possible. He's an artist. Babysitting could be an option. Being watched over by a tiger would make any child happy.

No. That isn't the Gene she knows.

"Ditch him," says Olivia, who isn't quite a friend but someone she can trust to a degree. "He comes to be fed and have sex, right? In that or any other order."

The summary leaves out so much. Being two.

"Right?"

Elaine nods, reluctantly.

"Do you sew on his buttons for him, too?"

"There's been no need. He wears his shirts unbuttoned, pretty much."

Olivia winces. "Ditch him."

If he hollers.

But he hasn't hollered, has he? He's just not been around a whole lot lately.

He wouldn't babysit. There is no child. Can't be.

Two weeks go by. Three. It's autumn now and after work Elaine busies herself washing and putting away her summer clothes, cleaning the windows, giving the kitchenette a thorough scrub. She considers buying heavy curtains for the winter, to keep out the draught. The warmth would be welcome. At the same time, their newness might entice the cats to start their climbing tricks again. She's in two minds.

It's rarely she gives Gene a conscious thought.

Four weeks.

That's when he contacts her, acknowledging that it has been a while. "Hi," reads his message. "Long time no see. How about tonight?"

No can do, she should reply. But she deflects Olivia's advice and welcomes him. This time, the first time ever, he brings sardines for Miriam.

They make love. The tiger, she notes, has paled – Gene's tan is all but gone.

She feeds him.

Casually, between mouthfuls – or such is her intention – she asks how he's been doing, avoiding the word 'what'. "Kept busy?" She pours more water into her glass, focussing on the task. Miriam, she notes, is watching him.

"On and off," he tells her. "You know how it is."

She doesn't, but he has shut the door on her. The only insight she has gained into his work concerns his story fragments. She tries to ease it open.

"And the child?"

The result is a blank look. Soundlessly Miriam sways her tail from side to side.

"The child," he repeats, but without a question mark.

"I took it you were babysitting."

"You did?" Again there's an extended pause before he continues. "Actually, there are two. Two girls."

"Your wife's."

"Yes." This time the pause that follows is quite short. "And mine."

"But I wasn't to know?"

"I'd rather not go into it." He pushes his chair back, gets

up. "As I said, I'm little more than a lodger."

Little more than. "A sort of" was the phrase he'd used before. How little more? Olivia was right.

"It's kind of you to help out with your children. Keeping your marriage afloat."

But why use sarcasm? It won't change anything. She watches him as he moves towards the hall. He gets into his shoes, his jacket. With his back to her he zips it up. He turns around. Hidden from sight, it is as if the tiger no longer exists.

"All good things come to an end," he says. He leaves the door to the flat gaping and heads for the stairs. Remaining in her seat, she listens to the echo of his steps, accompanied by the humming of a tune. He's never done that before. Could he be working on a song? As he reaches the ground floor, there is a squeaky sound followed almost immediately by a bang. Then all sounds cease.

Her tail held high, Miriam goes over to her bowl. She'll have her sardines now.

Some ten days before Christmas Elaine catches sight of him not far from where they first met. Walking beside him is a girl, too young to be his wife, too old to be his daughter. He has his arm around her and they kiss. Decidedly no daughter. She shrugs. That changes nothing. She is done with him.

And so, a week later, when her phone bleeps as she is getting ready to go home for her brief holiday, the staff party over, Gene couldn't be further from her mind. Seeing that the message is from him, she contemplates deleting it unread. Quite possibly he'd seen her in the street, observing him; kissing the girl may have been merely for show, to provoke her. Will he be texting her that there are more fish in the sea? Should she read it?

Curiosity gets the better of her. But if he had in fact seen her, he doesn't let on. What meets her eyes is longer than

97

anything he's sent her before and has the appearance of a poem rather than a message produced in a rush. There's even a title of sorts: "For You." Having glanced through it, she starts again from the top:

"So what went wrong?"

"Well, nothing, really. It just didn't work out."

"He didn't…?"

"No."

"What a shame. Still, you'd kept your flat, hadn't you?"

"Yes. And the cats."

"The cats?"

"Yes."

"You didn't consider…?"

"No."

"Perhaps you should have."

"I just couldn't. And then it was too late."

"How many…?"

"Why?"

"You're right."

"Anyway, I'm glad now."

"You are?"

"They're company."

"I can imagine."

"So is the dog."

"You have a dog as well?"

"It was his. He told me he liked dogs."

"And left it with you?"

"Yes."

"Good riddance, I would say."

"Yeah, I suppose."

She's puzzled. Is this meant to be her? She and who else? A casual acquaintance? Someone who doesn't know she has three cats? And what is she to make of it? Recalling his comments on very short texts, she counts the words and notes that with the title they add up to one hundred. One of his hundred-word stories. She is flattered, till she remembers that six words were a greater challenge. That takes away some of the glow. "World ends at noon." Still. The story is dedicated to her. In a manner of speaking. "To Elaine" would have been more of a tribute than "For You".

Arriving home, again with cat food in her bag, she finds a small brown and white dog, some kind of terrier, possibly part Jack Russell, tied to the banister outside her door. A tag bears the inscription "For Elaine". She sighs. Gene. But why? As if she, who already has three cats, could raise a dog – a dog which has to be taken out three, four times a day. She is a working woman. Having untied it, she picks it up and unlocks the door. She is met by Miriam, who arches her back. "We'll have none of that," she says, shooing her out of the way. "He's a guest." He? She?

Eeny, Meeny, Miny, Moe – that's who they used to be.

The janitor at work could maybe keep it in his room during the day, so she can walk it in her lunch hour. She'll have to give it some thought.

Whatever she decides, she'd better go slow.

Moe.

Erasing the past.

"Meeny," she calls. And Miriam steals up to her. "Meet Moe." And she puts the dog down carefully, shielding it with her arm. There. Just in case.

About the author

L. F. Roth has had stories published in competition anthologies brought out by Biscuit Publishing (2011), Earlyworks Press (2012, 2013, 2014, 2016), Bridge House Publishing (2014, 2015, 2016), Cinnamon Press (2016), AudioArcadia.com (2016) and Momaya Press (2016). They generally focus on relationships, gender issues and trauma – at times all three. For details and a few excerpts, see https://sites.google.com/site/lfroth1/.

Pambo Bwark… Glitter Chick

Dianne Stadhams

I hate birthdays.

In my family a birthday is a misnomer for a 'dead-darling' day. Whatever happens to other people on their birthdays doesn't work for us. We get a kind of upside down, inside out, back to front, reverse celebration. In my family when it's your time to have a birthday you lie down with cloves of garlic nailed to the bed, a fetish around your ankle and fingers crossed not to sleep… until it's all over… one way or the other.

"Garlic on the bed head? What next – elephant dung under the pillow?" my pa teased me on the eve of his 45th. He ordered my ma to remove the protection. My pa didn't wake up. "He's dead darling," said Ma.

And not just my pa. My uncle died on his birthday – bitten by a snake. My first aunt got out of bed, ate her birthday breakfast with an up-yours-darling smile… and fell sideways off the chair. They said she was dead before she hit the floor. The celebrations were cancelled. My ma said we could use my aunt's birthday cake for the funeral. But it took 60 hours from birthday party to burial pit. The cake got weevils. Nobody ate it. Ma fed the remains, weevils and all, to the hens. Their chicks were born with extra length feathers and super-wart wattles.

I could keep going as fifteen of my close family have departed this world on those bad days, their dead-darling days. My theory is that our family are mutants… with a genetic trigger alarmed for birthdays!

But this story is not about my family history and its genetic dysfunction. It's about a bigger big question – luck. A girl or a boy – who is the luckier? When a girl is born the old men in the village say to the father "Better luck next time!" My ma says to the fathers, "You are a lucky one. A daughter will be there to hold your hand when you die."

When it comes to dead-darlings it's evens on luck. The count changed with my sister's sixth birthday. Her best present was a pet chicken with long golden feathers that sparkled in the sun… and a red wattle with so many purple warts it was impossible to agree on the total. It was one supreme-ugly bird but she loved it on sight. Personally I would have denied ownership of something so hideous. But I digress – a birthday present is a gift after all. She called it Pambo which is Swahili for glitter. We all called it Pambo Bwark because it wouldn't stop squawking… very loudly. My sister carried it everywhere despite our taunts.

Party games like *Snap* and *I Spy* take on a whole new meaning when your sister gets eaten by a crocodile. The monster that lived on the nearby golf course got lucky with the chicken (a boy) and my sister (a girl… obviously). We don't know if it was a boy or a girl crocodile. It seemed to me that the croc scored top points with a double whammy birthday deal.

Eat one, get one free.

Nobody ate anything that day or at her departed-day ceremony. I guess there is no advantage in being a girl or a boy with a crocodile around.

I watched the grab and gobble fiasco from up a tree behind the bushes next to the water hazard. It was my first day of wearing the hijab. I was twelve years, three months and six days old.

"Today is your first-fortune day," my ma had said when she gave it to me to wear. "You are now a woman."

"Welcome," Ma's friends said.

Welcome? Worry is more like it! What if there is a connection between first-fortune and dead-darling days?

101

In DBH (days before hijab) I could climb a tree before my sister could count to ten. I always beat Urday. Urday says it's luck. But that's just Urday acting like he isn't bothered. Or trying to act chilled. Because Urday and me both know I am the better tree climber… and runner… and jumper-over-fences. Probably I am better than Urday at everything from school to sport. Which has to be more than luck as Urday is eight months, four days and fifty-eight minutes older than me. He is also three hands-stretched-open taller. Urday and I have been friends since my Ma and his rendezvoused beside the river with the other women in the village to wash clothes. Us turbo-charged, grubby kids went too. Fences and trees were our first challenges. The boys were fast but clumsy with bravado. The girls cautiously tottered in a bid for freedom. It was not luckier to be a boy or a girl on the move as your ma always caught you before it got really interesting. But Urday and I learnt that if you waited for a brother or sister to head off first, there was a degree of half luck as your ma chased a sibling before she got round to you.

And so I worked out that girls could create their own luck, whatever those old men said. But DWH (days with hijab) changed the odds. Tree climbing, running and jumping all took longer. And that's after you work out what you can see and where to run and jump – blinkered by a hijab!

When Urday turned up at my house wearing a hoodie my Ma was unhappy.

"A hoodie," she tuttered.

"Latest – like it?" Urday replied.

"No," said my ma. "What is wrong with what your father wears?"

She might be kind but she's definitely not subtle.

"Time for change," said Urday.

"Change does not bring luck," argued my ma.

"Maybe…" says Urday.

Yeah, whatever, like they're going to agree.

"Today is a day to take care and give thanks for our blessings. Today I have one daughter with six years of life behind her, and thanks be to Allah, six and sixty ahead."

"Happy birthday, little one," smiled Urday.

My sister showed him her present.

"Am I invited for a chicken dinner?" he asked her. She shrieked and placed Pambo Bwark under her arm. We all laughed. My sister loved Urday's joke.

"Today my other daughter is also blessed. Today she starts to wear her hijab," Ma announced proudly.

Urday looked at me and winked, knowing my ma was not looking. That wink was a challenge. He knew my luck had changed. The handicap had been granted.

"Hijabs cannot run as fast as hoodies," he whispered.

My sister started to run. Urday and I chased her. The game had started.

"That's hoodie hoodoo," I shouted.

Ma screeches, "Hijabs behave like women. Women walk."

So what about hoodies Ma? Do they have boundaries?

In DBH I might have been able to scramble down the tree and run faster. I might have been able to beat Urday to the crocodile. But that day I learnt that a hijab is not less lucky than a hoodie. For Urday got to the reptile before me. He ripped off his hoodie. He crept forward and threw it over to blind the beast. Confused the croc paused before tossing it off.

I screamed. I threw Urday my hijab. He lunged at the beast and tried to lasso the jaws with the sleeves of his hoodie and bind them as tightly as he could. The croc lashed its tail, trying to smack Urday sideways. But he was quick

103

like a flea and hung onto the tail – this way and that way. Urday hollered. I screamed even louder and longer.

Golfers – white foreign men – appeared, startled by the commotion.

"Bloody hell," said one of them.

"Mobile, give me the mobile phone," shouted another.

A third golfer ran towards Urday and the crocodile with his golf club. He smashed it down on the beast's head. Stunned the crocodile froze for a moment.

"Geez… it's got flesh in its teeth," shrieked a fourth golfer.

That's my sister you're talking about.

One man threw a golf club at Urday. He caught it. Between them they pulverized the croc's brain. The beast shuddered and stopped moving. What a scene – blood and brains splattered everywhere – on the ground, the golf clubs, the hoodie and my hijab. They saved Urday but not my sister and Pambo Bwark.

At prayers for my sister the Imam told us that those who are lucky to live have hope and those who have hope have everything. I told Urday that the best luck a hoodie or a hijab can have is a golf club or two.

Me and Urday plan to steal a whole set before I turn thirteen… just in case.

About the author
Dianne Stadhams is an Australian, resident in the UK, who works globally. She has spent many years in some of the world's poorest nations working on poverty-alleviation projects and has a PhD in communications for development. Her website www.stadhams.com gives details about this and her other interests.

Pictures at an Exhibition

Stuart Larner

The crowd quietened.

"So here, ladies and gentlemen, you see a line of ten large computer screens stretching down the hall." The acne on the art gallery attendant's face made him appear young and immature despite the dark square frame of his designer spectacles. "In each screen is a holographic reproduction of one of the ten paintings by Hartmann, which the composer Mussorgsky used for his piece 'Pictures at an Exhibition.' Please be careful not to cross the wooden safety rail, as the hologram screens are highly charged."

"Mummy, Mummy I can tell the time upside down." Thomas was swinging one-handed from the rail.

"No, you can't, that's silly," said his sister, Gabby.

"Yes, I can. It's eight five."

"You don't tell it like that," said Gabby. "That's silly. You say eight minutes past two. Have you been messing with your watch? Mine says three minutes past two. Look." Gabby held out her wrist to reveal the cheap pink-strapped children's watch.

"Calm down, you two," said their mother, Carmella, who was looking into the first screen in which a gnome walked up and down a country lane. "Wow. Look at that gnome's eyes, and he moves like he's alive."

"Yes," said the attendant. "That's right. All the characters are alive in their world of 5D technology. You have the three dimensions of space, the fourth of movement in time, and the fifth of solid reality."

"So it's like a computer game?"

"Yes. Only real. Inside the representation of the painting, the 5D means it can go on for infinity. Outside it, the envelope of that world is compressed into just the thickness of a modern monitor as you can see. There's no glass front, though. It's all held in by an electromagnetic layer…"

His voice tailed off and Carmella turned to follow his wide-eyed gaze as he looked past her.

"…Excuse me, madam, but will those children stop climbing on the safety barrier? That's very dangerous. It's highly charged and will draw them in if they get too near."

"Don't push me, Thomas!" yelled Gabby.

"I'm not. The computer's pulling me in."

"It's too strong! Mummy!"

Carmella watched in horror as the children's hands slipped off the rail. There was a large flash and an explosion.

When her eyes had recovered from the intense light, her children were no longer in the hall.

"What was that flash? Where are my children?" Her voice was high and stricken.

"I'm afraid they've fallen in." The attendant's eyes widened in horror behind his spectacles, his eyebrows rose in alarm. "You can see them in the mud down that country lane in the first picture. They're stunned."

"Gabby, Thomas!" Carmella screamed. "Come out of that mud at once! Do you hear me? You naughty children! I'll tell your father when I get you home!"

"They won't be able to hear you. We can see and hear them, but we won't be able to do anything."

"What? We'll soon see about that. Where's the emergency button?"

"There isn't one. To switch it off would destabilise the system and kill them. They're part of it now."

"Part of it? Oh my god! I don't like your attitude. I want your name and I want to see your manager. And, I want the police!"

"My name's Gregory, madam."

"Huh. And I'm Carmella Fortesque. My husband's a non-executive director of the gallery. So, listen. My children are in there. I want them out. Now."

"I'm afraid that isn't possible, madam."

"What? I'm not having this. I'm going in there to get them."

"I wouldn't advise that, madam. The adult human being would draw too much static to survive the barrier. You'd be killed."

"Huh! We'll see about that nonsense. Call the police, the fire brigade! I want to see someone in authority. Call yourself a museum attendant?"

"Madam, I might not know much about art, but I do know about computers."

"And not much even about that, I shouldn't wonder. Perhaps I can reach them with one hand."

"No, don't!" Gregory called, taking a step towards her.

"Gabby, Thomas, don't worry dears, Mummy's coming!"

There was another flash and bang, and Carmella fainted.

When she regained consciousness, the gallery had been cleared of people and her hand had been bandaged. "Oh, my hand! It burns! Who's bandaged my hand? Are my children out yet?"

"I did your hand for you," said Gregory.

"Where are my children? What's going to happen to them?"

"I'm afraid we don't know. There might be things hidden beneath layers from Hartmann's subconscious. He was a disturbed character. It's difficult to say which monsters lie deep in the mind of any artist."

"Difficult to say? Difficult…? I'll ring my husband.

He'll know what to do." She pulled out her phone from her bag. "Oh, there's no bloody signal!"

"I'm afraid you won't get a good reception near these machines. You'll have to go outside the building to use a mobile phone."

"What, and leave my children? No way!"

Carmella saw the children stagger to their feet in the 5D muddy lane.

They looked at each other, then about them, and screamed "Mummy!" repeatedly.

To her horror, Carmella saw the gnome limping towards them from the bottom of the display.

Gabby was afraid and started to run away up the lane, shouting for Thomas to follow her through a gap she had found in the hedge.

Thomas just stood there, mesmerised by the sight of the approaching gnome.

Carmella let out a gasp as she saw it brush against her son, steal his watch from his compliant wrist, and then limp off with it.

"What does it want with his watch?" asked Carmella angrily, affronted by the gnome's brazenness.

"I think to control time and to escape," said Gregory. "In a later picture there is a monster witch, Baba Yaga, in the form of a broken cuckoo clock. If she can restore herself, she can escape into this world."

"So, Thomas has to get his watch back in order to get out?"

"Yes, unless there's a way of hacking into the programme's coding."

"Can that be done?"

"It's very difficult, probably impossible. If you like, I'll try."

"Huh. I'd rather have a proper expert. Get your manager."

"He won't know as much as me. In fact, he's been

trying to get through to the help desk in Japan, but they're not answering."

Carmella watched the children struggle through the gap in the hedge, then they were gone out of the picture.

"What's happened? Where are they? They're gone! Oh no!" Carmella's voice climbed louder and higher. "Do you think this is a game? Where are my children?"

"Here," Gregory called. He was standing by the next display, 'The Old Castle'.

Carmella watched her children knock on the huge old oak door of an ancient Schloss.

The gnome had now appeared on the battlements and was pushing a large heavy stone over the edge. Gabby and Thomas were directly underneath, oblivious to the danger.

Thomas looked up at the last second and alerted his sister. They squashed themselves against the recessed front door as the stone came crashing down.

"I'll get you for this!" Thomas yelled at the gnome. He chased after him through the hedge into a field behind the castle. Gabby followed, shouting at him to stop and calm down.

The next scene opened into a park where a group of children played with sticks, surrounding Gabby and Thomas menacingly.

After being whacked several times, Thomas broke a branch from a tree, and began striking the children back. Gabby picked up a dropped stick and together they laid into the children in a ferocious battle.

Just at the moment when the gang were beginning to fight back and win, Thomas and Gabby saw a cart of hay coming into the park being pulled by an ox. Nimbly they jumped aboard.

Carmella turned to watch the cart pass into the next picture where it was surrounded by a group of strange beings. Each had a hen's head and was running around with human arms and legs sticking out of its hen's egg body.

"It's the Ballet of the Unhatched Chicks," said Gregory. "If they can get fully hatched, then they will be human."

"So, it's another instance of time stuck?" said Carmella.

"Yes. If the children come into direct contact with them, they might get stuck as well."

"This is ridiculous. What about the fire brigade, the police? If that witch manages to escape, we'll need a whole force here, not just a community constable," said Carmella.

"Yeh, but, I think the real answer is in the coding," said Gregory thoughtfully.

"So, what is your idea, exactly?"

"Well, you've heard of the internet of things?"

Carmella shook her head.

"OK. Well, the internet of things is where devices control each other without having to be told what to do by a human being."

"Kind of automatic?"

"Yes. That's right. Only this is the Supernet of Things. The world is now one big computer and anything that has a code can link into it and become part of it. And, with 5D, the Supernet can capture things if it recognises the code."

"You mean when the children fell in?"

"Yes. Except that I don't think they fell in. I think the computer drew them in."

"So, how do they get out?"

"I don't know. I'm going to try anything and everything. Write down all the numbers you know about them, dates of births, ages, heights, weights, significant dates, anything that could be used as passwords. I'll try typing them in and we'll see if the computer will cough the kids back out."

"Right, but in the meantime, where are my children

going next?" Carmella watched them get down from the cart and enter what looked like an old Middle-Eastern city. After walking along the narrow streets they came to a passageway barred by two sitting beggars.

"The painting of the Two Jews," replied Gregory. "These need help and the question is: whom do you help? One is rich, and the other is poor. But it is the rich one who is begging for more. And there are some coins lying in their begging bowls already."

"Well, my children are clever. They've passed all the tests so far. This is a no-brainer. They'll give it to the one who's asking for it."

"Hmm, I'm not so sure."

"But, yes. He's the more powerful. The rich one. They might have to pay him to get out. The poor one can't help at all."

Carmella watched as Thomas took coins out of the rich man's bowl.

"Thomas, what are you doing?" she shouted. "Those are the wrong ones. Put them back!"

As Thomas could hear nothing from the world outside the display, Carmella could only watch powerlessly as Thomas moved coins from the rich man's bowl to the poor man's. Gabby tried to stop him, but he persisted.

When both bowls were equal, a curious thing happened. Both Jews stood up to let them pass, and the poor Jew held out his hand. In it was Thomas's watch.

"Well, I wouldn't have thought that. He got it right!" exclaimed Carmella joyfully.

But her mood was broken when she noticed a red light beginning to flash on the console. She turned to Gregory who was typing furiously, and lightly touched his arm.

"Er, I don't want to alarm you, but what's that light mean?"

"It's a power warning," he replied, not taking his eyes

111

off his typing. "They're not normally lit up if things are OK, but when all three are fully on it means that the system is spent."

"And?"

"The computer shuts down."

"And? My children?"

"They, er, they disappear."

"Disappear?"

"Yes. They go."

"Go?"

"Yes."

"Go where?"

"Well, I'm afraid it's not good news."

"What!"

Carmella was stunned and was barely aware of the next display where the gnome had reappeared and chased Gabby and Thomas through a market place, trying to steal back their watches. The next scene was in almost total darkness.

Carmella shuddered when Gregory told her it was the catacombs, but she gasped with relief when the children appeared in the next picture safe at a clearing in some woods.

"I wouldn't be too pleased about that, if I were you," warned Gregory.

"Why?"

"This next is the Hut on Hen's Legs. The witch. See, she's in the shape of a Russian cuckoo clock hut on hen's legs. She's broken and needs to restore herself. But both kids are targets now, because they both have watches."

"Get them out of there! There's a second light started to flash!" Carmella screamed.

"Believe me, I'm trying." His typing faltered, then picked up a rhythm again.

As the children saw the witch, they were frightened and

started to run. Behind them they heard her cackling with evil laughter, "Come here my beauties. Don't run away from kind old Baba Yaga!"

"It's gaining," shouted Thomas.

"I don't know if we'll make it," feared Gabby.

"I'll throw it my watch. That's what the gnome wanted. Perhaps, the witch does too."

"Yes, and I'll throw mine as well. It's a different time from yours, and it might confuse her."

Two watches bounced off the roof of the cuckoo clock. It came to a halt, and then loaded up and struck one o'clock. The arms reached down to pick up the watches and then froze with a loud boing as some internal spring unravelled. It finished with a pathetic single weak cuckoo call as the cuckoo hung limply by a spring out of its window. The watches dropped in the mud.

"It's broken!" shouted Thomas.

"Don't stop," said Gabby, seeing it was beginning to stir again. "It's recovering."

"Head for the next gap, quick."

The children appeared in the final display, which comprised the enormously imposing Great Gate of Kiev in the middle of a deserted square.

The witch stirred again and Carmella, who had been watching with increasing horror, crept closer to the display.

"Keep away from the system," said Gregory. "You'll put yourself in danger again, and your children too."

"Now the third light has started to flash! Oh, my god! You've been no bloody use all along, have you? Admit it. Probably not in your whole life."

"You could be right. I've always hidden away with computers and programming. I can see that now." Gregory swallowed and looked down in shame. "And I haven't always been successful. I'm sorry."

"I'm sorry too. I've got no other option, now. And you've been a model idiot. Goodbye." Carmella stepped towards the display.

"Hang on! Did you say 'model'? Please let me try one last thing."

Carmella shook her head.

"I think it's something to do with the watches," pleaded Gregory. "Not the watches themselves, but the model numbers."

"I thought you'd tried all that."

"I've tried the times on the watches, yes, and the watches are now useless for anyone to use them as a key. But the witch studied them in some way and she is still heading towards the Great Gate. Where did you buy them from?"

"What do you mean, where did I buy them from? What kind of stupid question is that at a time like this?"

"Please, where?"

"Argos."

Gregory tapped on the console. "I'm Googling 'Argos catalogue on line'."

"What? You're seriously not going internet shopping when my children's lives are on the line and the third bulb is flashing? This is stupid. Now I know you're mad."

"Here we are 'Children's watches'. Which ones were they?"

"Oh my god! You are mad. You've finally flipped."

"Come on! Come on! Which?"

"OK. OK. To humour you. That one there with the pink strap. And one of the ones with the blue strap. Was it this? Or, no. No. This one, I think."

"Read me the model numbers."

"What?"

"Come on. Quick."

Carmella read the numbers and Gregory typed.

There was the noise of multiple locks opening followed by a clang and the Great Gate of Kiev swung back on its gigantic hinges.

"They're coming out, coming out!" shouted Carmella in wonder.

"Mummy! Mummy!"

They ran into her arms, stepping out full-sized as the gate closed behind them.

"Oh, my darlings. Here you are. You're safe."

"Mummy! We had a big adventure," said Thomas.

"Oh, is that what you call it?" Carmella laughed.

"They've safe now," said Gregory.

"Oh, thank you. How did you know at the finish?" asked Carmella through tears.

"The computer captured the kids because it recognised the code numbers of the watches and drew them in. Your children became associated with the codes. The witch wanted the watches to restore herself and escape, but got confused with them showing different times. Now, a big gate like that, I knew it must be a portal of some kind. Had to be that simple."

"Oh, thank you. I never knew that computer geeks were so wonderful and clever." She touched his arm. "I'm sorry for all the things I said."

"That's OK. I didn't realise I could do all that. I think I can now believe in myself a bit more."

"And Thomas, you have grown up from a boy into a little man – and Gabby, you have grown up into a young woman that protects her brother," said Carmella.

"Yes, they solved some really hard problems," agreed Gregory.

"And we didn't cry," said Thomas.

"Well, not much," added Gabby.

"I'm, I'm so proud of you both," beamed Carmella. "You've both grown up."

"Yes, and we've all changed for the better," pronounced Gregory.

"And that all proves I'm the best," smiled Gabby.

"No, I solved it all," said Thomas.

"No, you didn't," said Gabby.

"Did!"

"Didn't!"

"Did!"

"Changed?" sighed Carmella. "Ah yes, but how long will it last?"

About the author

Stuart Larner is a chartered psychologist. Besides writing for scientific journals, he has written articles, poems, stories, and pieces for the stage. He has published four books: *Jack Daw and the Cat, Guile and Spin, Hope: Stories from a Women's Refuge* (with Rosie Larner, collectively as Rosy Stewart) and *The Car*. He has a story in Bridge House Anthology 2016.

See his blog http://stuartlarner.blogspot.co.uk/.

Self Improvement

Michael O'Connor

Today, I am fabulously rich and unbelievably handsome, incredibly healthy and fantastically successful. I have a powerful memory and outstanding conversational skills. I fraternise with film stars and royalty, act as a consultant to several major international companies, and own an art collection which is the envy of museums across the world. I speak several languages fluently. I eat whatever I like without gaining weight, drink until dawn without ever suffering a hangover, and am automatically invited to every important social event. I never feel tired or listless. Men respect me and women love me. I can win friends and influence people without being in any way nice to them. My sexual skills are legendary, and in great demand. Household pets obey my every command and weeds never grow in my garden.

Yet just a few short years ago, I was a seven stone weakling. I had a dull run-of-the-mill stuck-in-a-rut job, dry unmanageable hair, and I used to get sand regularly kicked in my face by elderly ladies who carried some around with them for that precise purpose, as I was always too frightened of water to go near a beach. The computers in several dating agencies crashed when my personal details were fed in to them, rendering me persona non grata in those most romantic of places. I was an avid stamp collector and dedicated train spotter with leanings towards bird watching, although I have to admit that I never actually acted upon that particular avocation because I was afraid that too much exposure to the open air would harm my weak chest. My proudest possessions in those days were two complementary anoraks – one for best and one for day-to-day wear – and I enjoyed a case of acne which was quite astonishing for a man in early middle-age.

117

It was not a very rewarding existence and I was, to say the least of it, rather dissatisfied. Much of my ample spare time was devoted to scrutinising those seductive classified "self-improvement" advertisements in newspapers and magazines. I was constantly searching for a way to transform my meaningless existence without actually doing anything difficult or requiring the least effort or application on my part.

How, then, did I achieve the metamorphosis from wimp to wonder-man? Well, if you can spare a few minutes to read this true story, I shall tell you. You won't regret it. It won't cost you a penny. It could happen to anyone and you don't need to spend hours or days training or exercising or studying or doing any of the other tiresome things which most people foolishly assume are necessary to improve one's lifestyle. You don't need to do anything at all, in fact. My method for self-improvement is so simple that you will wonder why no-one ever thought of it before.

One warm June evening seven years ago I was strolling through the woods near my home, taking Buster for a walk. Buster was my next-door-neighbour's cocker spaniel, and he – my next-door-neighbour, that is, not Buster – was feeling a bit under the weather. Ever willing to be of assistance, and having nothing else to do whatsoever, I had gamely volunteered for dog-exercising duty. Hence, my uncharacteristic perambulation in the sylvan splendour of the local weald.

Though he had always appeared a docile enough beast in the presence of his master, Buster was proving to be something of a handful when he found himself in the charge of someone clearly inexperienced in the control of vigorous canines. Consequently, he had quickly cultivated a vexatious habit of running into the undergrowth where I couldn't reach him, and not emerging until I had given up hope of ever retrieving him and began to walk away, formulating a story of how he had been dog-napped by massive footpads, so as not to incur the wrath of his burly owner. On this last occasion, I had lost sight of him altogether, and spent over half-an-hour looking for him. It was getting dark and I was unsure if I could find my way back once the light was gone. I needed to get home fast. I was about to forsake the search and let the irritating hound remain in the woods for the rest of his life when I heard him barking in the distance.

With a muttered imprecation, I gingerly made my way through the thick bushes in the direction from which his yapping appeared to be issuing. Suddenly, something caught my eye: a flash of colour quivering on a dark green leaf. I thought it was a butterfly which had been hurt in some way, and went to look at it more closely. I had latterly been toying with the idea of taking up butterfly hunting; one would not have to go out in the cold to do it, and it was thus a less perilous activity than the bird watching to which I have already nervously alluded.

Imagine my surprise when I found, curled up on the leaf, a tiny female figure, naked and perfectly formed in every respect except that she had a pair of shimmering red and gold wings. I was even more surprised when the figure opened its eyes, looked up at me, and spoke.

"Oh bother" it said. "As if I didn't have enough trouble!"

"Whatever do you mean?" I asked, somewhat offended by this churlish reception. After all, I had only come over to make sure the creature was all right. And, possibly, to kill it, pin it to a piece of cardboard, and hang it on my bedroom wall.

"Whatever do I mean?" mimicked the tiny figure, getting to her feet. "I mean that you are a human being and I am a fairy, and I am not supposed to let you see me!"

"Fairies are real?" I gasped. She was indeed beautiful enough to be one, and although tiny, had an extremely attractive figure. With a pointed sniff, she curled her wings about her in belated modesty. I pretended to have been staring at the leaf.

"I am sorry to have disturbed you," I said politely. "I shall be on my way." I took a step or two towards the main path when the sound of stifled sobs halted me. I turned back. She was lying on the leaf weeping, her wings unfurled in wanton abandon.

"I don't like to leave a lady in distress," I said gallantly. "You mentioned troubles. Is there anything I can do to be of assistance?"

She stopped crying and looked up at me with a winsome smile. "Are you any good with monsters?" she asked innocently.

I cleared my throat uncomfortably. "What sorts of monsters?" I ventured.

"This huge beast has infiltrated our hidden camp," she told me. "I have been trying to lead it away, but it refuses to follow me. I fear for our Queen's life!"

Once again, she began to sob, her minute but shapely bosom rising and falling in a strangely appealing fashion. As I gazed at it – at her, I mean – I felt a wave of courage surge up within me, stiffening my sinews and hardening my resolve. "Lead me to this monster!" I cried, stiffly and hardily. "I shall save your Queen!"

The gauzy wings fluttered and she rose into the air. "Follow me," she instructed, and led me deeper into the forest, through thick thorns and barricades of brambles until we eventually reached a small sun-lit clearing which I had never seen before. It was filled with scores of tiny figures like herself, fluttering in the air and screaming in terror. And there in the midst of them, scampering and leaping, first at one and then at another, all the time barking excitedly, was Buster! "Is that your monster?" I laughed. "I think I can handle him."

I gave a whistle and called "Here Buster – dinner!" in a commanding voice. In a rare display of obedience for which I shall be eternally grateful – and eternity is literal in my case – the rambunctious spaniel halted in mid-leap and came to sit meekly by my side whilst I attached the two ends of his leash to his collar and to a propinquitous tree.

All the fairies had settled on branches and bushes and were watching me with undisguised awe. One, a little taller than the others, and disappointingly clad from head to toe in a glistening golden robe, glided through the air to hover a few inches from my face.

"Fairy Ann has told us about you," she said, in regal tones, clutching her robe tightly about her. "You are indeed a great hero. To show our thanks, we will grant you whatever your heart desires. As mere fairies, we cannot perform such magic ourselves, but we know this very obliging wizard…"

And that is how I became rich and handsome and healthy and successful and everything else I said. Anyone can do as I have done with no effort whatsoever. You don't have to work. You don't even have to log onto a website. All you have to do is find someone who can perform magic. Try it. You have nothing to lose!

About the author

Michael O'Connor has published two books and an e-novella and contributed to many anthologies, including four of the earlier Bridge House ones. He has had stories published in a large number of UK/North American print and online magazines, two of which received Honorable Mentions in the tenth and thirteenth annual editions of the Year's Best Fantasy and Horror. He won first prize in Writers' News Magazine's 2011 ghost story competition. His website is at www.mpoconnor.co.uk.

Silt

Christopher Bowles

There isn't any traffic.
...Why can't I hear any traffic?

The streets are too quiet. My footsteps clatter and echo off street walls like boisterous children. They simply don't sit still, ricocheting off into the dark corners and behind builders' skips. The cobble stones are uneven, and I have to make sure my feet don't fly out from under me; even though I'm not walking fast. Or with purpose. Directionless, wandering the city at night.

I heard if you listened hard enough, at the hour of witches, you could hear the city sing your name back to you.

My shoes are scuffed. Only slightly, from where I tripped on the stairs earlier that night. They are new. They are also pointier than the kind I'd normally wear – they make my narrow feet look even longer than usual; and when I first tried them on in the shop, I felt like a clown. But I bought them anyway. They were perfect, and they went with my suit, and I was really running out of time.

The laces are tightly tied, as if by my mother's expert hand. I recognise her handiwork all over my appearance tonight. The way I swept my hair back in a delicate slick over my crown. The way I starched my collar, and straightened out my bow-tie before the evening began. Even the simple manner in which I pulled out chairs for the ladies, and held open doors for strangers.

When one door closes, another opens. If all you see are

closed doors, find a window. Make one if you have to.

Tonight, I was very much my mother's son. She raised me well. I even ironed my trousers. I never iron my trousers. I made sure the pleat fell in just the right way, strong, yet not over-pronounced. I dug out that faded old suede bag filled with boot polishes and brushes. I made sure I sparkled.
I had to make a good impression.

When you leave this house you represent this family. I won't have the neighbours thinking we're common because you can't be bothered to tuck your shirt in…

She'd have me in the dining room by the ear if she could see me now. Shoes scuffed, trousers dirty at the knee. Shirt rumpled and hanging loose-edged over my pockets. Undone tie, its irregular design fluttering over two open buttons.

Of course, she never saw me when I'd been drinking. I was too much of a golden child to be caught with alcohol. But tonight, the party had been loud, and fun, and full of colours. I danced on top of a coffee table decorated in a montage of family photographs. I stubbed out a cigarette on the glass in the balcony door. I screamed with defiant glee over the city's horizon from the tiny platform seven storeys high, swinging from the railing. I necked bottles of beers, and stole unguarded glasses of white wine left on mantelpieces. I tasted three different shades of lipsticks. I threw fistfuls of glitter in the air and let it rain down on me.

Glitter still billowed out around me if I shook my head hard enough. My hair was full of it.

Don't forget to shine. Just be you.

Another crossroads. No moving vehicles. Just parked cars,

a parade of street-lights, a thousand soulless witnesses peering down from the factories on either side. Mannequins, I think. Perhaps harems of vagrants or forgotten equipment. Empty windows, broken panes. This quarter of the city was falling into disrepair. Mother Nature was taking the earth back in places – ivy choking the life from the old wood and stone. Moss creeping up brickwork in strangely regimented patterns. Mushrooms peering up from under tiny caps like toddlers. Brambles poking through shattered glass and pointing at the sky.

Only a fool looks at the finger.

I begin to realise I am not walking the way home. I am simply walking the city. I marvel at the fireworks painted across a low wall. Graffiti in purples and oranges and bone greys. It is beautiful, yet repellent. I reach out and stroke the mortar and I stumble on. This pilgrimage is taking me far, I know. But I have further to walk, longer to travel.

An underpass.

More graffiti. A white rabbit and a politician with devil horns. My suit is blue I think; and my head is throbbing – it feels too big. So I look for a bottle to make me small again. A can of cider, left next to a knotted plastic carrier bag and a used sanitary towel seems particularly inviting.

Drink me.

I snatch it up, and stagger to the next landmark, swigging deeply from it, and swilling the coppery taste around my gums.

A wind blows down the tunnel, and for a moment it catches me under my arms, and I am flying. There are no birds in the sky. I hold my arms outstretched, and let the breeze rattle between my fingers. I am surrounded by pink glitter again.

More graffiti. This time words. Messages.

"NO WAY OUT" they say.

"END IT ALL, YOU STUPID CUNT" in six foot high red letters. A fire exit sign sits on top of one the 'i's in place of a dot.

"OXIDIZED"... What does that even mean?

I don't know what the words mean.
...Why isn't there any traffic?

It looks like rain. Best wrap up warm today. I won't have you catching cold.

My eyes are shut tightly, and I'm back in the bathroom, snorting dirty snow off the back of the toilet, and focusing on that one single missing tile in the shower. I'm remembering twirling on the spot in the living room whilst the ambient music crashes over me in waves. I'm kissing that girl who has been watching me since I arrived. I'm studying photographs in the lounge, an older woman dressed in red hugging a small boy dressed in blue. I'm in the bedroom, and a man I don't know has my trousers around my ankles and my dick in his mouth, and I focus on the night-light and realise I'm in a child's bedroom. His friend watches from the doorway. Another drift of snow. Another twirl. Another tongue down my throat. Another photograph, another happy family. A speck of glitter in the corner of my eye. I can feel it, but I can't quite catch it with my fingernail.

When are you going to wake up?

Where am I now?

I throw the empty can into the bushes, and spark up a cigarette.

I breathe in the smoke deeply, letting it burn my lungs, just a little, before letting it simply escape from between my parted lips.

I am at a bridge.

Don't burn it.

Another drag from my cigarette.

No. Not just any bridge. I have never seen this bridge before. I have lived in this city for twenty years, and could walk for hours in any direction and still never get lost, but I have never laid eyes upon this bridge.

It is huge. A monstrous steel monument. The river below opens up impossibly wide, and it looks like it could almost be the ocean.

…Is it the ocean?

Have I walked all the way to the sea?

My, how you've grown. Let me look at you. You've gotten so big, lately. I can't believe how far you've come. It seems like only yesterday…

I stand at the dirty water's edge like a nervous child. I adjust my waistcoat. It seems so much colder now. Almost like the water itself were trying to steal the glow from my bones.

I look out at the horizon. And still, I struggle to figure out where I am. There are still no birds in the sky, no planes, and no smoke from the chimney stacks of the factories. There are no cars, no people, no sounds. Only my scant breath as I shiver, and clutch my arms around myself. I finish my cigarette and throw it at my feet, grinding it beneath my heel.

I cast a look back over my shoulder, back the way I came. There is a burnt-out limousine off to one side; a detail I somehow missed on my journey. In the middle of the road, there is a child's car-seat. In the car-seat, there is a teething toy – a white rabbit. It doesn't seem important somehow.

I look back out to the water.

The first step puts me ankle-deep, and it is cold. It is like fistfuls of needles all being jammed into one foot at the same time, and I want to cry out. But I want to be brave. And that keeps me quiet. A second step, and I'm up to my calf.

A definite audible gasp. A half-shout to pierce the deafening quiet.

Don't wander too far.

Hold my hand.

Stay near me, and don't let go until we reach the other side…

The water feels strange inside my shoes, and after another step or two, I'm aware of the drag. The pull back to the shore. The weight of the water. Up to my thighs, and immediately I wobble in place. Throw my arms out for balance, and gain my composure. I'm struck by the ridiculousness of the situation – I step outside of my own body to judge my own awkwardness. The boy in the clown shoes who thinks he's an acrobat. The next Houdini, perhaps? The boy who walked forever. The boy who ran.

The next step, and there is an unexpected mound on the floor of the water. A castle built on sand. It crumbles under my weight like the best laid of plans, and I'm up to my waist. My suit jacket is billowing out behind me now. My shirt bloating bizarrely with pockets of trapped air. I want another cigarette, but I can't turn back.

I know I have to keep going. So I keep going.

It's around my shoulders now. I hear the ominous creak of the metal bridge. I can feel eyes on my back from the shore. But I must press on.

Spin the bottle. Where will it stop? Who do you have to kiss?
Will they make you take your turn again if you get a boy?

Bring me the horizon! I march on, as only a drowning man can. I am weightless, even a single step is so much more effort than I'd planned now I'm up to my chin in cold water. My face feels like it is made of iron. My heart is pounding in my chest.

Come here.
Give mother a kiss.

I feel the first tear roll down my cheek as I plunge my face into the depths.

My hair plays about my face like smoke. I want another cigarette.

I wonder if there is glitter floating on the surface.

No way out.

The white rabbit watches from the bridge, twitches its nose, and my suit is still blue.

I can't hear any traffic.

Don't burn it.

I scream out over the city, and the city screams back.

I heard if you listen hard enough you can hear the night sing your name.

Listen. Repeat chorus.

Oxidize. Breathe. Heal.

A boy's best friend is his mother.

Why isn't there any traffic?

There are no birds, but there is a burnt out limo.

I want another cigarette.

Drink me. Snort me. Fuck me until my face feels like iron. Do everything I wanted.

When are you going to wake up?

My mother smooths my bow tie and presses down on my shoulders. Her fingers are colder than anything I thought possible.

I sink.

I miss you, mum.

The metal rolling thunder jolts me awake. The corners of my eyes are crusted and puffy. I've been crying again, and a half-empty bottle rests in the crook of my elbow. An ashtray spilling over with a mountain of stubs sits indignantly on the mattress beside me. I can feel my shoes are still on, but I don't care. I curl up into myself, letting the bottle fall to the floor. I clutch the sheets around me, and shiver to myself.

I struggle to focus; pick up a cigarette from the bedside table and light it. Inhale deeply whilst lying down. The ceiling seems to throb with cracks, and the uncovered bulbs swings in time to the rhythm of the passing train.

Breathe smoke into the air. Let the ash fall onto a piece of paper with a stranger's digits scrawled on it. Watch it start to smoulder. I wipe my face with the back of my hand, and lick white residue from my thumb; rub it into my gums and wait for it to kick in. I crave a whiskey, but instead I reach for the fallen bottle.

My hand stops, hovers.

I turn her framed photo face down. She never had to see her golden child like this. She shouldn't have to start now.

About the author

Christopher has been published in the previous Bridge House anthologies *Snowflakes* and *Baubles*, and has now established himself as a performance poet and playwright. Since having opened his company Magpie Man Theatre in 2015, he has seen award-winning success with debut spoken-word production *MOUTH*, and received critical acclaim for its physical theatre successor *AUTOPSY*.

This year he is set to introduce his one-man show *Live In Technicolor*, and continues his work as resident spoken-word artist with WWI remembrance choir *HONOUR*.

His collection *Spectrum* was published by Chapeltown in July 2017.

Snowstorm

Catrin Kean

I was at the bus station throwing chips at the seagulls. They screamed and spun around my head and the dog howled and people stumbled away from us all hunched like the sky was too low. A long time ago a charity lady came round with presents for everyone and mine was one of those glass snowstorms that you shake, and it felt like that now only better because now I was inside it with the seagulls and the dog and all of us whirly and blurred. But then Chappy came striding through and it was like bursting a pillow, the birds all blown into the sky. Chappy is big and loud with a face hairy as a coconut and he has that effect. The dog growled and slunk under a bench.

Chappy went, 'Hey girl, where you been all my life?' Which was what he said when I first met him, only then I was thirteen and I'd run away and I wasn't laughing, I was crying.

I don't cry any more.

I like it when he calls me girl.

He went, "Wanna come to a party?" That's what he said the first time I met him as well. I wished I had something better to do, but I'd ran out of vodka and I didn't, so I went with him. He held my hand and the dog dragged behind, a bit sulky.

We got on the bus and the driver went 'You'd better keep him on the lead,' about the dog and a woman glared at me and wrapped her arms around her baby hard enough to squash him which made me cross, making the baby scared for nothing because the dog's never bit anyone since I had him. But I didn't say anything because the woman was the type to talk back which would make

Chappy have a go and we'd end up getting kicked off the bus.

We sat at the back on the engine which made me feel sleepy and sick and Chappy chatted and I looked out of the window at the warehouses and the dockland machinery and the train yards and the brown river and the muddy horses snatching at the grass under the flyover. I remembered this girl in school who used to come on the mitch with me. She smelled sweet and secret like a proper girl and plucked her eyebrows and straightened her hair and I didn't know why she wanted to be my friend but she did. We used to sneak out of school and go and look at horses and feed them handfuls of torn grass and warm our hands under their manes. And one day we got on one, me in front and her behind with her arms tight round my waist and I grabbed a chunk of mane and we dug our heels into its stomach thinking it would buck us off but it didn't, it just galloped off up the field smooth as a rocking horse. We shouted at the sky and clods of wet mud flew and my friend's hair whipped the wind. Our thighs bare against the horse's rain-soaked back.

Chappy asked me what I was thinking, which was that her family found out about us going on the mitch and said she wasn't allowed to see me anymore. She tried to talk to me about it but my sister said she wasn't worth it and told her to get lost.

I said to Chappy, "I want a horse."

"I'll buy you one," he said, and put his arm round me and his clothes smelled of earth. I watched the horses until my breath had fogged them over and then we got off the bus.

The party was in the Fight Club that isn't a fight club any more. There's still part of a wooden sign hanging over the door that says MARTIAL AR S, which means Chappy makes the same joke every time we go there. Inside there's a hall with mats that are all stained and chewed like the mice have a go when there's nothing better to eat. The place is owned by Dan who lives in a caravan next door. Dan is always sad and never says anything. Chappy's the opposite: Chappy never stops talking.

Well we went in and it didn't look like a party to me. I'm nearly seventeen and I like a good time and this wasn't it. This was just Dan and a bunch of winos passing a bong around. I like uppers. I can get myself down just by thinking about things and I don't need to stick my face in a plastic jar for that. I wished I was back with the seagulls or watching the horses on the bus. But Chappy rubbed his hands together like this was the best party ever and we sat down on a mat and he gave me the bong first because he's a gentleman like that.

I said, "Isn't there any vodka?" and he went, "You don't want to drink that crap, it rots your insides," and then he gave me the look that he keeps hidden behind his smile.

"Take it." So I took it and I breathed in the sweet bubbly smoke and for a moment I felt like I was flying and then I felt sick. I told Chappy but he didn't answer because he was inhaling it himself. Then he nodded, his spiky red face all happy, smiling at a secret in his head. I got up and he grabbed me: "Where you going?"

"I feel sick," I said. 'I hate that stuff.' He tried to pull me down and I told him to get lost. But he doesn't like it when I talk back so he punched me. Bells rang inside my head and the dog looked up a bit concerned but didn't do anything. The winos watched us with half-closed eyes, their eyeballs rolling in their heads.

Chappy said, more to them than to me, "I'd like to fuck you now but…" He smiled at the bong and spluttered, his eyes all watery. 'This is the shit. My dick's not up to it. Sorry baby.' The winos sniggered, all stoned and high-pitched. Actually Chappy's dick's never up to it anymore, but I wasn't going to mention that with the mood he was in. So I just said, "Well you can all do that to yourselves if you're clever enough." And I called the dog and went to the caravan. There was no light in there but I found the bed and got in and the dog came in with me, all heavy and quiet.

My first time was in this bed, in that other party when I was thirteen. I felt sick then as well, but that time Chappy came in with me to make sure I was ok or so he said. I knew he wanted to do it with me because of the way he looked at me and I didn't mind, you had to do it sometime, but I didn't think it would be this time because Dan was there. But Chappy took my clothes off anyway while Dan watched with his face all droopy and sad like a clown. I thought Chappy might kiss me or something first but he just put a condom on and went straight in. Behind the Fight Club there are railway lines with the trains rocking and moaning up and down and that was how it felt, like a train going into me. I bit my lip to stop myself screaming, but Chappy heard me sighing and thought he was doing it good. Then he wanted to do it again but he didn't have any more condoms so he went into the hall to get some more, and I heard him go, "This girl's hot, she's going to keep me up all night." And Dan let out a sigh and I felt like a girl in a song.

Chappy only used condoms when he could boast about it to the others so pretty soon I was up the duff. I wasn't going to do anything about it, I thought it would be nice to have a baby and dress her up and do her hair and stuff, but my sister found out and told my foster mother who told the social and they said I had to get rid of it. They said if I didn't it would get took off me when it was born anyway. So I went to the hospital and they asked me all about dates and I didn't know so they did a scan and they turned the screen towards me and I saw my baby all tiny and with a hand up to her mouth like she was waving. I think they did it to punish me but I thought it was lovely and I couldn't believe I could make something like that and before they stuck the needle in me to make everything black I gave her a name which is a secret I'll never tell anyone.

This time, I woke in the early morning and me and the dog were still on our own in the caravan. The lace of the old curtains was like scribbles against the grey sky. The sheet I was lying on was all stained and I didn't want to be there anymore. I got up and everything hurt even though Chappy had only punched my face, but when you get punched like that your muscles go tense so it feels like you've been punched all over. I tied the rope round the dog's neck and we left. We walked through the hall and nobody noticed us: Chappy and the winos looked like waxworks, all happy and lost in the fog.

The fields behind the Fight Club were flat and scrubby. Black and white horses slept standing up and the pylons wailed above our heads and there were skinny trees with plastic bags flapping from them like leaves. The estate behind us was quiet with everyone sleeping in, which is why I like Sunday mornings the best.

Near the railway line there was an old brick building and I sat down behind it so that if Chappy did come looking he wouldn't find me. I looked at my arms which had little green and blue marks on where his fingers had grabbed me and even though I don't cry any more I felt like it then because I knew I would go back to Chappy even though I didn't want to. The dog was barking at the building and at first I told him to shut up but he kept on so I got up and went to see what he was barking at.

There were no windows inside. There was water on the floor and it stank in there. I stood in the doorway, the dog whining and straining on his rope. As I got used to the light I could see something, pale, moving a bit, like an image on a screen. I told the dog to keep close and I paddled through the putrid water and I saw that the pale thing was a horse.

She watched me coming, her eyes all wide and white. She couldn't move her head very far because she was tied up with a head-collar that was too small and that was cutting into her skin. I moved closer saying 'Hey hey,' all soft and calm so she wouldn't be scared. Underneath her raggy coat I could see the shadow of the inside of her, her ribs, her spine. I put out my hand out and she blew her warm breath on me and I moved closer to touch her and then I saw it, curled and perfect in the stinking water at her feet. A white foal.

The dog sniffed at it and the horse jerked her head and kicked out at him but the foal didn't move and then I knew and bells rang in my head like when Chappy hit me. I tied the dog up and then I touched the horse's head on the bony bit above her eyes and then I ran my hands under her mane down to her back. I could feel her breath moving in and out and her frightened heart. I touched her until she dropped her head. Which meant she was ready.

I untied her.

She nudged at her foal, breathed in the smell of it.

"Give her a name," I told her, and she stayed with her head down over the foal for a long time and then she looked at me again. I untied the dog who was whining and straining on his rope. I told him "Shut up and behave yourself," and we all went out. The horse threw her head up at the light and tried to back into the building again but I said "Hush, hush," and I stood with my back to her. The thing with animals is that you've got to give them time to understand that you're not going to hurt them. Like with the dog, I got him off this bloke who'd kicked him around a bit, so when I got him we sat for a whole day, all quiet, just next to each other, and I let him decide when he wanted to be friends.

So I stood there and didn't look at her and I could feel her thinking behind me, working it out, and when she stepped out of the building I walked and she followed.

It was still hazy and early but people were waking up. A few cars drove through the estate and on one of the fields a minibus was parked and boys in football shirts were clambering out. I got scared in case somebody saw me, in case her owner saw me. The horse walked carefully, blinking in the white light.

I took her to the stream where there were some trees so we were a bit hidden. The water was slow and brown with car tyres in. She grazed her mouth across the surface but then swung her head up and breathed the wind. Thinking. That's what I like about horses. They think, a lot.

I picked handfuls of grass and tried to feed them to her. She took a bit but not much. There was dried blood under the head collar but I had to leave it on. I thought about taking her to the Fight Club but I didn't trust Chappy and the winos with her. I've got a vet card for the dog so I can take him for free, but if I took the horse to the vet they'd know she wasn't mine.

We walked along the railway track and there was an old man in a grandad cardigan and baggy trousers standing there with his back to us, drinking tea from a flask. I didn't want to go back the way we'd come so we tried to go past him but the horse stopped and wouldn't move and the man turned round. He had pale rings around the outside of his brown eyes and wrinkles that looked like someone had drawn maps on his face.

The horse reached her head out and smelt him.

"Your horse?" he asked. His milky eyes made him look kind.

"I rescued her," I said. "Just now."

She was still reaching her head out to him. He held out his hand and she blew on it.

"Someone didn't treat her right," he said. "You get her somewhere safe now."

Safe. It was a nice word. Somewhere her owner couldn't find her. Somewhere Chappy couldn't find me. I said it out loud: "Safe." And then I realised there was somewhere, not for ever but for now.

I wanted to say thank you to the man but he had turned away again. I looked back as we walked away but he was drinking his tea and watching the tremble of the train track and he'd forgotten us already.

My sister's house backs on to the flat fields that run along the river. She won't let me in the house now I've got the dog; she's proper phobic and thinks he's going to eat the baby. But I remembered she'd gone on holiday for a week, Corfu or Crete or somewhere. I pushed open the rusty gate. There was water collected in the trampoline and the horse tried to drink from it but I pulled her away because it was dirty. I smashed the toilet window and squeezed through. I filled the washing up bowl with water and brought it out to her.

My sister's always cleaning in the house but she doesn't bother with the garden and it was waist high with grass and dandelion leaves and the horse chewed a bit. I pulled the rope off the washing line and tied the horse with that instead of the other short one so she could move around, but I didn't want to take the head-collar off in case she got out through the hedge. I went back into the house to find something I could use instead of the head-collar.

If I had a house it wouldn't be like this, all white with flowery cushions and curtains, but my sister's got this thing where she has to keep cleaning. That's why the garden's all messy because she won't let the baby play out there because of the germs. I looked at some photos of them on the mantelpiece, her and her husband and the baby, all smiley with a blue sky and clouds behind them which wasn't real but painted onto a curtain. On the wall there were framed photographs of flowers and sunsets with writing on them, things like 'A ship is safe in harbour but that's not what ships are for,' and 'Only in the darkness can you see the stars.' I couldn't see anything I could use for the horse though so I went upstairs. My sister's bedroom was all girlie pink and the baby's was blue with white clouds painted on the walls, but there was another room at the front which was more messy, where she kept her hair straighteners and stuff. She had some shoe boxes piled up in there and I opened them and had a look through. My sister's always making cushions and curtains and there was sewing stuff and lots of ribbons and fake flowers and I put my hand in and felt down and I felt something round and hard.

My snowstorm.

There was a Santa inside it with a reindeer pulling a sleigh. I shook it and the snow whirled around and the thoughts in my head whirled around the same. I thought about a tiny pale hand on a screen and I thought about Chappy's fist and my face stinging and I thought about bare thighs on a horse's rain-soaked back and a girl's secret laugh on a day that I was happy.

But mostly I thought about my sister and that she took my snowstorm.

I thought the horse would be afraid coming into the house but she didn't mind. I fed her apples and carrots and breakfast cereal from a glass bowl and then I brushed her matted coat with a hairbrush and pale hairs broke away and floated in the air. She watched me and I could see myself in her eye.

I gave her a secret name and told her she was mine.

About the author

Catrin Kean is a Welsh writer who is working on her first collection of short stories. Her work has been published in Ripside Journal, Bridge House Anthology 2015 and The Ghastling. She has been awarded a Literature Wales mentorship and a Literature Wales bursary, and in 2016 won a place on the Literature Wales/Hay Festival new writers' scheme 'Writers At Work'. She currently lives in Cardiff.

Storm in a Teacup

Deborah Rickard

Joe genuflects in front of the altar, fingers flicking a cross over his chest. An act of habit? Or is his dedication as sincere as the day we married in St Cuthbert's?

And how about our dedication to each other?

I saunter up the aisle, gazing at the myriad frescoes crammed into the spaces between overhead vaults. Now that really *was* dedication. Some 13th century artist had lain on his back, pushing up close and personal to the ceiling for aeons painting those. Lovingly nurturing each finely wrought detail and fighting any temptation to give up. I find the effect, though, somewhat oppressive and wonder whether he'd been obsessed with inconsequential detail. I pull deep on sanctified air, chill with the rot of age, and join Joe at the altar.

It wasn't intentional; what happened last month at the Medico-Surgical Spring Convention. I'd hardly thought about David since we left medical school some twenty years ago and went our separate ways – he to the north to pursue his career and I to the south to pursue mine. He was listed as one of the speakers but when you see "Dr D. Jones" on the programme you hardly notice. As a consultant radiologist it's my job to look beneath the surface but one of my failings in life is only seeing things at surface value.

Or not even bothering to look.

Joe and I stroll in single file back down the aisle to the narthex and a shelf laden with leaflets detailing the history of yet another ancient parish church, another manorial stronghold, just like the one we'd visited the weekend before. And the weekend before that too. Probably.

Not that we're regular worshippers. Visiting country

houses or churches has simply come to form part of the routine we've fallen into, like Joe locking the door at night and me taking the tray up to bed ready for early morning cups of tea. Often, like today, our excitement is twofold, with a grand house *and* a church tucked discretely into a corner of its grounds. We've seen so many surely there's nothing more to learn?

Back outside we wend our way around crumbling gravestones, crusted with lichen and crawling with ivy. We wander through the lych-gate into a tussock-ridden field, Joe thinking of I know not what and he equally unaware of my meandering thoughts. Neither of us bother to ask these days.

David's touch triggered a charge that day we met again, and his eyes locked on mine as if he was CT scanning my inner depths. "I was hoping you'd be here," he said.

Beyond the ragged field sits the house, graceful and serene, surrounded by linen-pressed lawns, rose terraces and knot-gardens of close-clipped box attempting to confine swathes of loose-limbed lavender within its rigid frame. The sky stretches wide and blue above us but the Cotswold air hangs close and heavy, the birds absent and the leaves on the trees unmoving. A stagnant silence wraps around Joe and me, so tight the giggle from a couple in the distance cuts up close and personal, catching my breath and piercing my heart.

Joe and I used to laugh like that.

So where had our sparkle gone? The sparkle which had glittered like stars in the shower of confetti on our wedding day?

I turn to Joe, lost in his own world, and back again, to mine.

Over the years all David has been to me is a momentary memory over cappuccino in a café when I'd seen someone vaguely similar at another table.

"Cup of tea?" Joe asks.

Well it *is* four o' clock.

We amble across the long grass towards the house and its neatly ordered garden. Rabbits scurry off into the meadow bordering the field; left to seed and dancing with cornflowers, ox-eye daises and a host of scarlet poppies. A sigh escapes from my chest.

A week after we met again David drove for three hours to buy me lunch and give me roses. He asked me to leave Joe and move up north with him. I can see his roses now, as red as those dancing poppies in the next field but bent and forlorn; pushed into a rubbish bin on the Brompton Road because I couldn't take them home for Joe to see and ask questions. I still haven't given David his answer. And Joe has no idea.

But wait! Poppies… dancing?

Yes! Bright red poppies frolic in a frantic frenzy with blue cornflowers, yellow and white daisies, and tall, tango-ing grass. High above this colourful confusion, petals swirl skyward in a dusty haze, ducking and diving like cavorting lovers spinning higher and higher in pursuit of some ultimate ecstasy…

But how? The grass Joe and I tread lies still and somnolent, and the trees, too listless to lift their leaves, hang languid in the afternoon sun. Joe notices too and we stop.

"A whirlwind!" he exclaims. "And it's coming closer!"

We stand, transfixed by the spinning spectre veering at an angle across the meadow and pushing towards the oak on the edge of the field. The vast, indomitable tree rustles in a lissom shimmer like cymbals flashing on a tambourine. Leaves flee from its branches to soar with the spiralling ballet while the grass beneath tugs this way and that in a bid to join in.

143

This strange phenomenon steels silently towards us and I clasp my hair in one hand while my other reaches to stay my swaying skirt. Joe turns to face me and our eyes meet; holding fast on one another; puzzled, amazed.

Excited?

The wind gusts and buffets in our ears. Joe's eyes narrow in the cutting bite, his nose wrinkles and his cheeks crank into an uneasy smile. I let go of my hair and feel it fly around my face. I let go of my skirt and feel cotton billow and caress my waking my skin. I reach for Joe's arm to steady myself and feel *his* skin; warm, firm and familiar. And together, in the dust and wind, we laugh.

We laugh out loud.

It passes in a moment and we move on for tea; dust and petals, like faded confetti, clinging to our clothes. And a sparkle lingering in our eyes.

About the author
Deborah Rickard trained as a journalist in the 1970s and some years later, after raising her children in Bristol, she took up writing again while studying for a degree in literature. She has since had short stories published in print magazines and anthologies, and two short monologues performed by the Bristol Show of Strength Theatre Company. She now lives in South Devon where she writes and paints.

The Crystal Gazer

Cathy Leonard

Mildred Moody opened the shop door slowly, hoping to avoid the tomb-creak that usually ensued. She dodged the chimes that somebody insisted on hanging at eye level just inside the doorway. A glance at the notice board told her that Somebody had rearranged it again. First of the month, every month, some insistent body reorganised the business cards. Mildred would now have to scour through row upon row of them in search of her own, just in case Somebody had decided to shred her this month.

She closed her right eye and screwed up her left one. That way she could make out, eventually, the gold rimmed edges of her own business card, almost obliterated by a brash rainbow offering of Indian Head Massage, Reiki and cellular healing.

"I left yours up, Miss Moody," chirped a voice from behind the cash register – Tara, the owner's teenage daughter, headphones in situ, painting her nails black, tuned to Spin 103, while Terry Oldfield poured tranquillity around the shop floor.

"You should move those chimes," grunted the little woman in the second-hand Mac and down-at-heel Clarks Springers and clutching a Tesco bag-for-life.

"Magda says the sound of chimes breaks up stagnant energy, Miss Moody."

"Your mother may be right, but somebody will lose an eye!"

That said Mildred turned towards a shelf arrayed with precious stones and crystals. Glittering amber, carnelian and obsidian winked at her from glass bowls. A particular amethyst caught her eye. In its polished face she could just about make out what might be the head of a hyena God. Anubis weighing hearts at the time of the passing over. Anubis trapped in a crystal time frame!

Mildred felt for the coin in her coat pocket. Her fingers swept the expanse of pocket lining until they encountered an unexpected gap in the seam. Without moving her head Mildred looked sideways at the girl behind the counter. Tara was talking with animation on her mobile.

"Bored – speechless. Two customers – all day. Weirdos! Guess who's here again?" The voice dropped. "Yeh, the loop. She's seeing visions, in stones! Says they talk to her. Yeh, I know!"

Mildred's fingers crooked and burrowed deeper into her coat lining. Just as she reached the edge of a coin the chimes rang out and Mildred lost contact. A young man in a business suit and pink tie blustered in.

The amethyst was winking furiously at her. She turned her back to the counter and reached for the stone. The business suit was checking out the CDs.

"Temple of the Forest? It sounds relaxing, but is there any water sound in it? I hate the sound of water."

"No idea," the girl replied.

"Perhaps I could hear a track or two?" the suit persisted.

Mildred heard Tara's sigh.

"Call you back in a sec," she said to her friend on the mobile.

"Are these ionisers any use?" he queried.

He was going to be a problem.

"I'll find you a leaflet." Tara vacated her perch behind the cash register.

This was Mildred's chance. With a deft move she bagged the amethyst.

High heels clip clopped behind her.

"Can you put that stone back on the shelf, Miss Moody!"

"I can't, as a matter of fact. It's probably stuck in the hem of my coat. Besides it was an experiment in energy transfer…"

"I've heard it all now!"

"If you attune yourself to the crystal it can be moved along any axis, Tara."

"Well then, I'd be grateful if you would attune it back to the shelf."

"Attunement uses up a lot of energy, my dear, and, for the moment, I'm zapped."

The girl's painted nails tapped with menace on her hip bones.

"She'll pay you next time," came a voice, apparently from Mildred's pocket.

The tapping stopped. The business suit dropped the salt crystal ioniser that rained orange splinters onto the shop floor.

"You heard Anubis! I'll pay you next time." And Mildred, negotiating her Clark Springers through the salt crystal shards, headed for the door. Chimes rang out as the door creaked to a close.

The high heels headed for the notice board, and the black painted nails prised out a gold rimmed business card that read:

Mildred Moody
Ventriloquist and Crystal Gazer
Fortune Teller and Soothsayer.

Holding the card ceremoniously between painted thumb and forefinger, Tara picked her stiletto steps through the glittering glass strewn across the shop floor. At the back of the shop she opened a door and leaned over a toilet bowl.

147

The nails released their prey and the card fluttered into a swirl of flushed foam.

"It's called bullshit, Miss Moody!"

About the author
Cathy has been writing and teaching for over thirty years. She has published poetry, short stories and children's stories and has been shortlisted for a number of awards, most recently runner up in the *Fish* Flash Fiction Award 2013 and the *Sceine* Poetry Competition 2014. She had a short story selected for publication in *Baubles* 2016 and has been participating in the Café Lit project. Cathy lives in Dublin with her husband Stephen, Molly her trusty red-setter cross and their new arrival – a stray one-eyed ten-month-old kitty, Sherlock. Now all they need is a Watson!

http://bake-a-yarn.blogspot.ie/

The Girl who Sings for her Supper

AJ Humphrey

They hunted my brothers to extinction – the old man and his people, with their gunpowder and hounds. Far away from the big old house they drove me: beyond the wide sloping lawn and the fairy ring, the high lichened wall with its razor curls of wire. I am Reynard, and I am the last of my kind. But they could not keep me away for long.

Through the bars of the black iron gate I creep. And I know you've seen me from your high, narrow window. You watch as I slink a slender shadow across the lawn, ears cocked for sense of danger. You wonder who I am, and why I'm here.

You're the girl who sings for her supper now. You've grown up on quails' eggs and ewes' cheese, on spring water mixed with hot milk and spiced with pepper to help you fight off the chills. It's clammy in the big old house, as the dampness fastens her crafty, crumbly fingers between the stones and round the roof-beams. The old man lights a crackling fire in every hearth to keep the chills at bay. The servants are weary from their foraging, bowed like old trees under the weight of wood they've scavenged from the ruins of what used to be the forest. The damp has got into their bones too. They smell of it. The house smells of it.

I haven't forgotten the child you: how you used to let me watch as you sat at the window and brushed out your hair, ready for bed on those long summer evenings when the light seemed to last forever. You used to wave to me, blow me kisses. I think you barely remember me now. I'm a shadow on the lawn, the ghost of a memory you can't quite summon. But I never forgot you.

This is a world without birdsong now. The old man and

his kind have left us a ruin of a kingdom. Black silhouettes of lime and poplar, lining the driveways of their estates. Skeletons of hawthorn, branches scrabbling against the stones of their everywhere walls. The linnets and goldfinches have left us in droves, looking for faraway lands where the grass is as green as it used to be in our childhood, the berries as ripe and bright. Tar and concrete cover the acres where my mother used to play as a girl. The air has an oily taint to it.

That's why he keeps you here: locked away behind the high wall. This sloping lawn with its fairy ring and its springtime speckle of crocus, it could be the only green in the kingdom, for all you know. The brief riot of leaves, that comes before the burning sun and the storms, the only colour. He's trying to preserve it here. A time capsule of what he's lost, of what he and his people have stripped from the earth.

You learned to sing as the birdsong faded. I remember you trying out your voice, the reedy girlish thing that it was. Singing to me. Now you sing for your supper. For the scraggle of sheep in the enclosure, chewing at the bristled branches of the empty hedge. For the quails in their pen, pecking and scratching their lives from the grit, the fall of dandelion-seed. For the few small, sour apples that outlast the storms, the nutmeg and cloves locked away in the old man's safe.

Did he tell you it was all my doing, this withering of the land? The old man was lying. He's lying to you still.

I've seen what the old man never will. The colour of sunset over shadows of mountains, the brightness of dawn light shining on the sea. And I know a secret that the old man will never know.

I know that we are fighting back. Nature. The grass. The linnets and goldfinches. And me. For I am Reynard, the last of my kind. I can take you to places far, far beyond this old rotting house. Far from the old man, from the servants who creak like leather as they bow to you. And I will show you such sights as will make you sing for joy.

I can show you the place where the goldfinches and linnets have gone: beyond the ruin of this kingdom, where the grass still grows green and thick. Where a thrumming of bees and butterflies crowds the waving heads of a million bright flowers, and the air is thick with their perfume. There are oceans and cloud forests, mountaintops teeming with hares.

I can take you to the city too. The city is loud with music; the pulse of the crush of people is her heartbeat. I can show you ballrooms full of ladies in sparkling gowns, and their stony-browed lovers, wreathed in cigar smoke and mystery. And in the secret corners, where no one notices, I can show you the cracks in the concrete where the grass is beginning to grow through once again.

It won't be long now. I know this old house from my childhood, and I know how to pick locks. There are secret passages that the mice and beetles have shown me; passages through the servants' quarters, behind the hearths. Gateways. I will pick my way through the dying embers, come to your room when the old man is asleep. We'll escape together, you and I. Over the wall and away.

It could be a hard life, the two of us out on the road: the girl who sings for her supper, and Reynard, the last of his kind. There will be dangers. Men who smell of gunpowder. It's true that from time to time you might give a sigh and a backward glance towards the narrow window, the wide slope of lawn and the fairy ring, and wish yourself back here. I know that if you truly wish hard enough, I'll never be able to hold you back. But first you must see the world beyond the high lichened wall, and know what the old man

151

has been hiding from you, all these years. You must taste the fire in whisky and kisses, the salt of tears. You must learn a new music, the pulse of the resurgent earth. A new dance, that I shall teach you.

I am Reynard, the last of my kind. And this is my promise to you.

About the author

Andy Humphrey is a legal adviser by day and a poet by night. His writing uses images from nature, myth and fairytale to create contemporary narratives of love and loss with an undercurrent of social comment. He is the author of two poetry collections: *A Long Way to Fall* (Lapwing, 2013) and *Satires* (Stairwell Books, 2015) and has appeared in the Bridge House prose anthologies *Making Changes* and *Spooked*.

The Litter in Glitter

Linda Flynn

A flicker of light glinted through brooding grey clouds as Rose pulled the rumbling bins behind her. The park. A perfect start to her day, somewhere peaceful, with only the stirring of bird song.

She speared up the litter, careful to straighten her back to avoid a stooping ache.

A bin spewed out some half eaten sandwiches, broken pieces of blue plastic, a baby's dummy and some broken glass. Lucky that she had found this litter before a child had stepped in it, or fatally a puppy had run off with a small object in its mouth.

Rose gazed upwards through the web of branches of an old oak tree and pulled down a flapping plastic bag.

The yellowing sky opened its spotlight on the park as it slowly awakened. A blackbird hopped upon a twig, the gate creaked open and a swish of bike tyres sped along the path.

Bruised clouds bunched together again as she completed her circuit. As she neared the groaning traffic, the air became clogged with fumes and her bins filled quickly. After the first drop off point she had to cover both sides of the High Street. In her regulation fluorescent yellow jacket and grey waterproof trousers with the luminous stripe, she felt fairly anonymous, sure that people would look through her. Even so, she felt a flutter of fear at recognition.

In the take-away quarters, she scraped up some old rice and dog's mess, but had to leave some chewing gum which would need to be blasted off the pavement. Shattered pieces of glass lay in pools, winking in the remaining rays of the sun.

Rose looked at the purple clouds and pulled up her hood. Leaflets fluttered in the rising breeze and she struggled to capture them. One escaped and slumped soggily in an oily puddle. She paused when she saw the crimson heading of, "St Benedict's Art College." In her gloved hand she read, "On 1st April at 19.00 talented students will be holding an Art Presentation on stage to an audience, instead of at a roam around exhibition. The local media and companies have been invited." Details of obtaining tickets followed as Rose pummelled the limp leaflet into her glove.

Once again she recalled how her fingers had been poised to knock at the studio door. Her mind was sparking with ideas for the exhibition and she longed to share them.

Her hand dropped to her side. Through the rectangular grids of the safety glass she saw him with his back to her, his arm around an animated woman.

Her soul sunk. She stood transfixed. The woman gave a tinkling laugh and shook her auburn hair as they both turned to look towards the doorway.

Rose turned and ran, her breath coming in shuddering gasps. She had to escape the truth, to put some distance between her and them.

In the past she had not minded the age difference; he was her lecturer and she had been flattered. Of all the students, he had noticed her, nurtured her talent, shown her that she was someone special. She had glowed in his spotlight.

Rose's eyes hazed over when she reached the railway bridge. All that she had left now was her pride. The canvases that he had praised, the compositions that he had encouraged, all were left behind. She never wanted to see them again.

Now she felt as though she lived in a vacuum, without colour or brightness, sludge grey.

Rose shuffled forward and elbowed a loose strand of hair out of her eyes as the first drops of rain fell. She tried to tug her hood further over her eyes as pedestrians scurried past, registering her presence no more than the pigeons at her feet.

Under a shop's canopy she scooped up the sludge which had spilt from a rancid pot of yogurt and a squashed, putrid banana. The bins smelt of festering fish and made the shoppers turn away.

It was the shoes she noticed first, the red sheen daintily avoiding the puddles as they scampered to find shelter. Rose faltered. Her heart stopped. The couple froze. Rose saw his electric flicker of recognition. His arm was held lightly around the woman's waist.

She dipped her tawny head towards him and pointed. "Isn't that the girl you mentioned? You know, the one who suddenly dropped out of your Art course?"

His brows furrowed, immediately to be swept away by a closed-in face as he shook his head and turned away. The woman who appeared to be his wife tapped him on the arm and persisted, "I'm sure it's her – all big canvases and grand ideas. Left suddenly as you said she couldn't cope with the demands of the course!"

Rose did not wait to hear the rest. She stabbed a squashed sandwich with her litter picker and crushed a coke can underfoot.

The rain slid over her hood and ran in rivulets down her flushed cheeks. Despondently she trailed her debts and disappointments behind her, like the black bins.

Her gloved hand slipped as she tried to grasp a glass bottle, which spun in an arc through the air, before shattering into jagged fragments. She stopped. She stared at the prisms of light refracting off the sharp edges. In that moment she knew what she had to do.

Once Rose closed her bedsit door at three o'clock each day, she cocooned herself in her own creative world. In her hand she held a piece of charcoal and used sweeping upward strokes across sections of newspapers.

At night her head flew across the pages, swirling upwards, higher, further, straightening, before a flourishing finish; her world was entwined in an intricate web.

She straightened her back, flicking her hair back behind her ears, examining the shapes from every angle.

Every day her mind planned, visualising the details; each evening the threw herself into the expression, firing her body into frenzied activity. Jewelled colours flowed through her hands, dripping in showers of sparkling rain.

Rose knew she was ready.

Her heart thudded as she stood outside St Benedict's College, dragging her bins behind her. She felt sick. Rose took a deep breath and pushed open the swing doors. At the back of the darkened hall she waited.

Some muttering arose from the students when her name was announced. She had deliberately registered her place on line at the last moment, relieved that her Department of Education number was still valid.

She took a deep breath and stepped forward, dragging the grumbling bins, before carefully lifting a black plastic bag from each one and placing it on the stage. The background laughter and conversations seemed to blur in Rose's head as she stepped on to the stage. She reminded herself that not only students and lecturers were seated in the darkness, but potential sponsors.

Rose moved forward on to the centre of the stage, enveloped now in silence and flanked by three large plastic bags. Someone from the back called out, "Look! She's brought all her rubbish with her!"

Rose let the sniggering subside, before fully emerging from the shadows. "Yes, that's right. I have." She had captured their attention now. "Everything I will show you this evening has been made almost entirely from recycled litter and natural materials that I have found."

She eased herself back into the darkness and slipped off the first black bag. Silence. Her heart hammered. She flicked the switch.

The lamp spun a golden pool of light into the gloom. Its shade was a bird poised for flight. The driftwood neck which was embedded with a glass mosaic, was outstretched. Its delicate shell beak was reaching upwards, the ruby glass eye gazing fixedly towards the charcoal sky. Behind it streamed a fan of feathers, each one made from intricately coloured paper clips, opening into plumes of saffron, russet and burgundy flames.

Rose let the Phoenix dance its way across the ceiling as the audience gasped, then she extinguished its fire.

Next she lit up an underwater world with blue green swirls dancing above and around the audience. Fish fins made out of plastic spoon heads, coloured with iridescent nail polish, flitted through wafting weeds, driftwood and shells – opalescent flashes in an inky gloom.

Rose paused before revealing her final lamp. There was a collective intake of breath. An oak stretched out its branches in an arc which encompassed the whole room. The tangle of twigs twirled into a tracery of spindly sticks, with glass green leaves glinting like sprites.

She flicked the switch off and stood still in the darkened room, holding her breath.

Only when she heard the roar of applause did she enclose herself in the centre to reignite the Phoenix,

Underwater and Woodland Worlds, so that she was enshrined by the glowing lamps.

As Rose stepped off the platform she knew that whether she found a sponsor or not, she would find her own way towards a glittering, creative future.

For Tina, Nicky and all those people who voluntarily pick up litter.

About the author

Linda Flynn has had two humorous novels published: *Hate at First Bite* for 7- to 9-year-olds, and *My Dad's a Drag*, for teenagers. Both won Best First Chapter in The Writers' Billboard competition.

She has six educational books with the *Heinemann Fiction Project*. In addition she has written for a number of newspapers and magazines, including theatre reviews and several articles on dogs.

Her short stories with Bridge House include: four adult stories, *To Take Flight*, in the *Going Places* anthology, *I knew it in the Bath* in *Something Hidden*, *Snowdrop* in the anthology, *Snowflakes, All That Glitters...* in the Christmas 2016 anthology *Baubles*, as well as *The Wild Ones*, for teenagers in *Devils, Demons and Werewolves*. Two children's short stories: *The Secret Messenger* and *Timid Tim* were included in *Hippo-Dee-Doo-Dah*.

In November 2016, Linda also had a satirical short story, *Wake Up Call*, published in the CaféLit best-of anthology and *Poppy a Puppy for Remembrance* was placed with CaféLit in April 2016. Both of these were published in The Best of Café Lit 2017.

Linda's website is: www.lindaflynn.com.

The Lone Valley

Clare Weze

I knew immediately. That first day, before I even got my suitcases upstairs I knew it was a mistake. At the interview, she was just like she is on telly, and it was mega-quick, in a posh Mayfair hotel. All smiles she was, like when she's reading the news, but when I got to her house in Chelsea a week later, it wasn't her any more. She was someone else. Same face, but with… issues.

And I messed up. Her real name isn't what you hear on telly. It's Madelaine.

"*Laine*," she said. "Not *lin*."

We were in the kitchen and she was giving me what she called *orientation*.

I tried to be friendly. "Wasn't there a song called Madelaine? K D Lang, was it?"

"That was *Chatelaine*," she said, and she didn't look too pleased. "I hear you're quite a cook, Amber."

She'd talked to Susanne, who I babysat for when I was still at school. Susanne can overdo things. Well, what was I supposed to say? I'd given it plenty of welly at the interview, so had to follow through. Interviews are a farce anyway. Everyone knows you just tell them what they want to hear.

I tried to turn into what she wanted, but my cooking wasn't poncey enough. And anyway, I don't see how you can be expected to keep a whole massive house clean and make something for tea as well. And she had people round to dinner loads, so it had to be perfect all the time, like a Spring Clean job. She did the cooking then, but I had to help and I didn't understand what she was on about half the time. She called things funny names and used

159

weird stuff. *Quince paste. Candied orange peel.* Where was I supposed to get those, and how would I even know what they looked like? I worked out that if I bought couscous and coleslaw and green gloop from the deli and put it in one of her fancy glass serving bowls she was cool, but when people were coming, she wanted a banquet.

One time she got all embarrassed about me standing serving, and made me grab a plate and tuck in. But I wouldn't thank you for an olive. I don't think slimy blobs taste nice just because someone else says so. And can I help it if I don't like stinking blue cheese? Felt a right idiot standing there with a plate of posh crisps, but it was fun too, in a weird way, listening to everything they said. Same load of bollocks over and over, till I could hardly keep my face straight. But then she introduced me around, and *they* started watching *me*. They looked at me strange, like I was something from another world.

One massive bloke tried to get me talking about the shipping forecast, as if I'd have a clue.

"If they scrapped it, Radio Four audiences would beat down the doors of Broadcasting House and set about the staff," he said, all elbows and nose. He'd cornered me at the kitchen table, which had ultra-vile red leather seats built into the woodwork, like a booth. Leather in a kitchen: it's just wrong. Too much steam.

"Ha, yes," I said, and all the skinny women in Boden dresses tittered with their heads on one side like I was twelve. Thighs on them no bigger than one of my arms.

"I don't think I should be hanging around here now," I whispered to Madelaine when I got her on her own.

But she wasn't really listening. She never listened

properly. Too busy swooshing that shiny dark bob and planning what she was going to say next. You wouldn't think so to look at her on the news. She looks like she's listening when she interviews people, doesn't she? Suppose it depends who she's talking to.

She had us eating together most nights. Table set, candles lit, the lot. I think it made her feel all fair and liberal. But the next minute, it'd be, *Amber, you mustn't leave the dishcloth hanging over the tap*, like she'd told me ten thousand times before – but she hadn't. Made me wonder how many people had done this job before me. Then she'd reach round and run her fingers over her disgusting leather café seats and I'd used the wrong cleaning stuff on them, and why hadn't I been listening? I hadn't to mess with the coffee beans – leave those to her; I was always putting the Sellotape back wrong; OMG, it was like being back at school, except that sometimes, she put her arm round me all motherly and I'd think, oh, she's all right really. But then she'd start on at me again. Hot and cold. Can't stand people like that. If you like someone, you should like them all the time and be straight with them.

Should have jacked in then, but where was I going to go? I'd burnt bridges. Packed in my flat and the job at the pub and I wasn't going to give any of them the satisfaction of seeing me crawl home. "See if you can hold this one down, love," my nan said. I always listened to her; the only one of the lot of them that ever treated me decent.

And anyway, there was London. On my day off, London was my big reward. I walked for miles. Found my favourite places: the glittery lights reflecting off the Thames at Bankside, and the Millennium Bridge. And I found out that 'The City' is an actual place inside the big city. I used to wonder what people were on about when they said, "I work in *The City*." It's different there. Hardly any proper shops, but the buildings are dead tall and it all looks Victorian. I quite like that. I started to go off shops a bit. I changed. Started looking for something different. Even kept hold of one of those flyers they hand out in the street, for a cocktail bar. Even went there one night on my own. And it was all right, as it turned out. Bit of an adventure. Dark bar full of candles, mirrors on the ceiling turning the tiny flames into a million glittering stars. Jazz band playing in the far corner, softly, like a mirage in the background. And as I walked towards the bar, the music climbed higher and higher – especially the piano – and it felt like they were doing it for me. Felt like this was it. This was the place.

Should have stuck to that kind of adventure, when I look back. When I tried to tell Madelaine about the magical atmosphere and the glam, sparkly people that could have walked straight out of a painting, she said – and I still can't believe this – I should be careful next time in case they thought I was on the game!

One day not long afterwards, Madelaine said, "Amber – your workload is going to increase dramatically."

I just stared.

"Yes *please!*" she said, as if I should be grateful. It was always like that. *Your workload*, as if I was a secretary or something. *Prioritise your tasks, liaise* with the deli, and *keep the lines of communication open.* That just meant telling her things.

So anyway, I made a blooper. Would have told her as soon as it happened, but whenever I went to her with stuff, she blathered about me *developing resourcefulness*, especially since she changed my job and my *workload* went *through the roof.* Great how people do that, isn't it?

162

You think you're going for one job and it turns out to be something completely different. Not that I minded at first. It was just a bit of easy office stuff. Emailing to thank people for crap from a copy-paste template she'd set up. Deleting spam that got through her junk folder. But this was on top of the beds, the cleaning, the laundry and the cooking. Didn't get paid a secretary's wages, neither.

It was an email, just like all the hundreds of others, about a charity gala, or some such farce. How was I supposed to know it wasn't for passing on? *Passing* them *on* was what I'd been told to do.

Had to sign as her PA, not her housekeeper, and wasn't supposed to file them in proper email folders called normal names that anyone could understand. She filed them by date, then when something new came in on that topic, everything had to budge up one. Never worked in an office, me, but I couldn't have dreamt up a more twisted filing system if I'd had a century to do it in. Tried to tell her that – nicely – but she was having none of it. Me, have an idea that might be better than one of hers? You have *got* to be joking.

Anyway, I forwarded it to everyone on the gala list, like I'd been told. Then the replies came in.

She screamed at me. "Didn't you read it?"

Well I'd skimmed it. Some nerd wasn't to sit next to some other nerd. That's all.

Thought she was going to sack me. Left me hanging for a few days and there was a worse atmosphere than usual, but then it blew over and we went on holiday. It was spring by now.

"We're going to the Lune Valley," she said. Well, I thought she'd said the *Lone* Valley, with her flutey mouth. Thought we were going to end up in Death Valley when she

163

said she'd be driving us. Needed to get her head down for a while, apparently.

It rained all the way there. She had Radio Four on and for once, it didn't bug me. In fact, I enjoyed some bits. Especially the shipping forecast. Especially picturing the places, and the rolling waves and lighthouses. It made me feel wild and sleepy at the same time. Cromarty, Forth, Tyne, Dogger. Fisher, German Bight. Faeroes was best. I could have gone for that. (Even googled those places later, and they're not all where you think they are.)

"So lovely up here," she said when we got settled. "Look. You can see the clouds scudding across the moon, Amber. No buildings to obscure the view."

I looked, and it was pretty, but what's 'scudding'? Nobody says 'scudding'. I don't think it's even a word, is it? Ponce, always ponce, with her. Loved the silence though, halfway up that hill. I'm from Birmingham. I'm not used to wilderness. And the blackness outside, and the stars. No streetlights, you see. Reminded me of Cromarty and Faeroes and all those high, wild places.

Sheeting it down again in the morning. Felt like we'd come to a house in the clouds. But when that cleared out and I saw the view down the valley, I sneaked out to the garden before she woke up, and leaned against a tree that looked older than old. Deep ridges in the bark. I spewed clouds of breath out at it. Told it stuff. Told it Madelaine had crooned on the phone to one of her squeezes last night, about how she wanted to be alone for a bit. *Better alone than badly accompanied*, she'd warbled. Only she wasn't alone here. She was with me.

Could have sworn I heard it whisper back. The breeze blew my hair up lightly, tickling, and rustling the leaves right next to my ears. *AMBERRRR...* Madelaine came out and sat on the skanky old bench by the front door. Too rickety to take my weight, but she perched on it sipping her tea, like an actress in a scene.

Wouldn't think you'd need your housekeeper/PA on holiday, would you? Not normal. She had me cooking and tidying and ironing just like always. Everything she wore still had to be washed and ironed the day after.

The second day she said we were going down to the town. Well! Some town. Kirkby Lonsdale it was called. Blink and you'd miss it. Cute place, though. Olde Worlde. Saw a really buff lad buying his dinner in the bakery. He looked a bit dusty, probably a builder, but that was cute too. Like he was dusted with icing sugar.

Two days later, I saw him again. Madelaine had let me catch a bus. "Get some more provisions for the cottage," she fluted, "and take some time for yourself."

Said he came from a place called Hutton Roof. The Dark Side of the Lune, he called it, and when we both laughed, I really felt like something might happen.

But on the way home, I got a text. My nan was in hospital. She'd collapsed with her kidneys.

When I told Madelaine, she didn't spout out at all. Nothing. Not one thing! Most people would say "sorry", at least, but she didn't even say that. Might as well have told her my dog was at the vet's.

She gave me an order instead. "Could you blitz the marinade ingredients, please?"

All narky, as if she was the one with the poorly relative.

"Erm, I really need to go to her. My nan."

Everything went quiet.

"Go? Where? Your next day off is Saturday. It's up to you where you go then, but at the moment, I need you here."

"But it's only Wednesday. I've got to get to her before Saturday."

"You said she was on a ward."

"Yeah?"

"Not a high dependency unit. A ward. It doesn't sound as if she's in immediate danger, so the weekend will be plenty of time." And she walked off.

Hot and cold, see. No more, *Ooh, Amber, look at the scudding clouds…* Iceberg time, now. Just like that.

My heart went whumph, whumph, and all the blood rushed to my head. Felt like I might have a heart attack. Bitch. That's all I could think.

Upstairs, though I thought clearer. I could see the sheep munching away inside their barbed-wire walls. No more rooftops anywhere around, just me, her and the sheep. Me up here, mad as hell. Her downstairs, being a bitch. I knew what I had to do. There wasn't even a choice.

The laptop was in her bedroom. I took it into mine and was logged in inside five seconds.

And yup – I took my revenge. I forwarded all her sent emails to everyone in her address book. Every single one. Didn't take long. Dead simple. And this time I read some of them properly, and they were cracking.

Like this: *You've got to watch Mia. She's one of Lars's winged monkeys.*

And this: *Please don't tell Stephen about our conversation with Lucy – he thinks Lucy is in Cardiff.*

So, yeah. I doctored them. Then I packed my stuff and did one. Because leaving the house and catching twenty-seven thousand buses and trains to Birmingham meant walking out on her, which meant not being paid what I was owed without a fight, which rich bitch would win.

Sweating like a donkey by the time I got down the hill and out of sight of the house, but it was worth it.

About the author

Clare Weze has been writing fiction for most of her life, starting as a child, and writes both for adults and children. She is a Northern Writers' Award-winner (2016) and a runner-up in Unbound's 2016 short story competition. Her work received a special mention in the Galley Beggar Press short story prize (2016), was longlisted in Fish Publishing's short story contest (2016/17), and will appear in the next Bath Flash anthology (2017). An extract of one of her forthcoming children's books is to be featured in Commonword's anthology of 'children's writers to watch out for'.

Her short fiction has been published by Bridge House Publishing and Curiosity Quills Press. She is also the co-author and editor of *Cloudscapes over the Lune*, in aid of the children's charities Make-A-Wish Foundation® and Rainbow Trust.

http://clareweze.com/

The Party's Over

S. Nadja Zajdman

"Madam," the operator stated, "you'll have to end your call. You have an incoming call from a gentleman named Laurie, and he says it's an emergency."

"What?!"

"Madam, please disconnect your present call. I'm putting the gentleman on the line."

"Laurie, what the hell?! Why did you get an operator to cut into my line?!"

"I'm sorry, I had to do it." Mark's mother was almost as excitable as his own, Laurie thought. "I'm on the emergency ward with Mark. There was an accident." Hearing a scream coming, Laurie hurried his words. "But he's O.K. he's O.K. He got hurt in a hockey game."

"Oh my god! My boy! My poor boy! Where is he? Is he conscious? Can I speak to him?!"

"Sure. I'm about to bring him home." Mark's foot was in a cast, and he was supplied with crutches. Laurie handed his buddy the receiver of the pay telephone on the emergency ward.

"Hi Ma."

"What happened?!" Mark and Laurie winced as Mum's piercing wail ripped through the receiver.

"Nothing much, Ma. I stopped the hockey puck with my foot. The doctor says I have to stay off my feet for the next 24 hours, that's all."

Realizing her son would live, Mum recalibrated. It was Friday evening. Daddy and I were out shopping for ingredients for tomorrow night's party. Laurie was put in charge of the guest list, since he knew Mark's friends. It had been originally arranged that Laurie would keep Mark out of the

168

house the next day, so we could prepare for the party. The next day was Mark's birthday, and I was arranging this surprise.

Daddy and I returned from shopping before Mark and Laurie returned from hospital. "Sit down, Abram," Mum commanded, "and don't panic. I have to tell you something." She did.

"Vot?! Why is Laurie in the hospital with him and not me? Why didn't he call me?!"

"He probably didn't want to upset you, Daddy." I knew my brother well enough to understand his motives. "Laurie would keep cool, and be able to help him better."

"Hunh!" Feeling rejected, Daddy grunted. "I'm the father. *Mein* son is suppose to call me!"

The next question was, how on earth were we going to prepare a surprise party if the recipient of the surprise wasn't able to leave the house?

"We'll manage," Mum lifted the grocery bags Daddy and I had brought in and carried them into the kitchen. "We'll just have to work around him."

When Mark hobbled into the apartment, assisted by Laurie, he was pointedly ignored.

"Why did you use your foot to stop the puck?" Daddy asked, incredulous, as he and Laurie helped Mark into his room, relieved him of his crutches, and helped him into bed. "Why didn't you use your head?!" Daddy's crack was meant to mask his anxiety. As far as Mark was concerned, it didn't succeed in doing so.

Laurie joined Mum and me in the kitchen. "There are twenty people expecting to ring your intercom tomorrow evening around seven. What should I do?"

"Call them and tell them to stay away," Mum directed.

"You're going to cancel the party?"

"No no. Tell them to meet you downstairs in the lobby."

169

Generally nervous and impatient, Mum was masterful in a crisis. "When we're ready, you can bring them up. And here," she tossed Laurie a package of deflated balloons. "Take care of these. We can't put them up if Mark is here."

"Ma." I turned to my take-charge mother. "When and how are we going to bake the cake?" The odour of a cake baking would instantly arouse suspicion. Mum was a tigress when it came to protecting her cubs, but she wasn't cut in the *Betty Crocker* mould. Baking and cooking were luxuries reserved for women who had time for them. Mum's energies were poured into working beside Daddy in the business they built together. Daddy was proud of his helpmate. He would brag, "Vot *mein* wife makes for dinner is – a reservation!"

"We'll have to do it after Mark goes to sleep," Mum decided. She was already splitting and pitting the purple-skinned, yellow-fleshed plums.

"In the middle of the night?" I was aghast.

"Maybe."

"Of all the days." I shook my head and wielded a small pair of scissors, snipping and separating bunches of blue-black grapes. "Mark has to stay off his feet for one day, and tomorrow has to be the day."

"Kiddo, it's a communist plot." Mum had done with the plums, and was coring Cortland apples. "But a good communist keeps going!"

Daybreak found Mum lighting matches and waving them around the kitchen, in order to diffuse the odour emanating from the stove. The plum and apple cakes were cooling on the counter. Mum left the kitchen and knocked on Mark's bedroom door. "Sweetheart, are you awake?"

"No!" From beneath a thick quilted blanket, Mark moaned.

170

"Well you are now!" Mum burst into the room and extended her arms. "Happy birthday, my darling! Gimme a hug!"

"Ma, I can't." Mark extended his bandaged foot.

"Oh, right. Well, if Mohammed can't come to the mountain…" Mum sat on the edge of Mark's bed, leaned over, and kissed him on the forehead. "What a beautiful morning!" She beamed, as sunshine filtered through the blinds and beamed with her. "My son is 21 years old today! Now if there's anything you need, you let me know and I'll bring it to you. How about breakfast in bed?"

"Sure Ma." Injury had its perks. "Can you bring me a glass of orange juice, and a bagel with cream cheese?"

"If we don't have it, Daddy will go and get it for you. Now you just stay put and we'll take care of everything." Mark's room was located directly across the second bathroom. He needed to go no further, calculated Mum. My room was located at the far end of the apartment, off the kitchen and dining room. That's where the evidence would be stashed.

A tray of sliced, pungent cheeses was wrapped in *Saran* and hidden behind my typewriter. A bowl of plump grapes, both green and blue-black, was covered with a linen towel and tucked under my desk. Puff pastries, perched on the separated dividers of a silver serving dish, were balanced on the windowsill in my bedroom. Once the plum and apple cakes cooled, they were placed on large platters and slipped under my bed.

Mark, remaining in his pyjamas and a bathrobe, his injured foot propped on a chair, spent the day studying at his desk. Obligingly, he kept his door closed. Still, he heard the patter, and through the crack at the bottom of his door he could spy the movement of three pairs of functioning feet as

171

they crisscrossed the apartment throughout the afternoon. Just before six o'clock Mark limped into the hallway. According to Mark, Mum and I seemed to have grown heavier during the course of the day. My caftan and Mum's housecoat proved poor disguises for the finery we had on underneath. Daddy was still in casual dress, but then Daddy was always in casual dress. Little short of a wedding or a funeral could compel the old socialist to put on a tie.

"I'm hungry!" Mark called. "Can I get something to eat?" Mum and I were setting up a buffet at the dining room table. We nearly leapt out of our respective caftan and housecoat. "Anything you want! In a minute! We'll bring it to you!" Mark grinned. My brother was a good lad, and a bright one, even if he had stopped a hockey puck with his foot. "O.K. I'll wait." His grin spread, like the Cheshire cat, and he removed himself to his room, leaving the mice free to play.

The party was set for seven o'clock. It was almost seven-thirty and, except for immediate family, the apartment was ominously empty. "I'll go downstairs and see what's going on," Daddy volunteered. On the main floor lobby of the apartment building, nineteen young people huddled on the steps, party horns in hand and at the ready. In a far corner Laurie's girlfriend sat quietly, her lips pursed and her cheeks puffed, intently blowing up and tying multi-coloured balloons.

"Laurie, why is everybody still downstairs? We can't fool Mark much longer." As if Mark had been fooled, at all.

"There's one guest missing. We're waiting for him."

"Why? He can find our name on the panel," countered Daddy, logically. "Come outside with me. I've been cooped up all day. I need air." Our cozy corner of North America was on the cusp of autumn and winter. Daddy stepped outside, in his shirtsleeves, anyway.

"But its cold outside!"

"Oh you big baby! So vot! It's healthy! It's good for you! Come outside!"

Shamed into it, Laurie obeyed. Man, but Mark's father was tough. At that moment a red Porsche, its radio blaring rock music and its headlights blazing in the dark, careened down the street and skidded to a halt. A short, sandy-haired young man with a grin like a chipmunk hopped out, on the driver's side. His leggy blonde girlfriend tossed her golden mane, flashed her toothy smile, and emerged from the passenger side.

"Hi Laurie! I'm here!" The Porsche's owner hailed.

"Who the hell is that?!" Dad's half-bare arms flailed in the chill night air.

"That's Marty." With his girlfriend Leslie, Laurie failed to add. "Mark met him last summer, in camp. Marty was Mark's supervisor. He was head counsellor."

"He's late." For Daddy, lateness denoted disrespect.

"Oh, Marty is always late." Already, those in Marty's orbit accepted that the rules which applied to them did not apply to him.

"So that is Schwartz's grandson." Daddy had heard of his son's new friend. Mark had mentioned him a bit too often, for Daddy's comfort. Marty was the scion of wealthy *parvenus,* and heir to a textile empire. Daddy was aware of the family's shady reputation in business. A mischievous twinkle lit his soft brown eyes. His wife wasn't on the premises to recognize the warning light, and stop him. "Get outta my way." Before Laurie could think, he had dutifully stepped aside. The heavyset, middle-aged man stomped his feet, like a horse, spit into his palms and rubbed them together, then sprinted down the street and leapt onto the hood of Marty's red Porsche. "Hi!" Gleefully Daddy leered at Marty, who stood stunned. "I'm Mark's father. I'm here, too!" Daddy began to bounce on the car's hood and slap at it with his palms, eyeing Marty all the while. "Let's see how strong is this car. Let's see how much pressure it can take." Marty stood paralysed. Leslie stood transfixed. Laurie was no longer surprised by Daddy's pranks. He knew that, at some point, the man's motives would be revealed.

"Hok Kay!" Daddy leapt off the car, never letting his gaze leave Marty. "Looks like this car can take it!" Daddy extended his hand. "How do you do!" Marty raised his palm and dropped it limply in the older man's hand. Daddy slapped Marty on the back so heartily and shook his hand so hard that the younger man nearly toppled over. "So you are coming to the party?"

"Yes sir," Marty muttered.

So come on in!" Daddy marched vigorously into the apartment building. Marty glanced furtively at the hood of his car, checking for scratches. Then he, Leslie and Laurie followed the leader, in silence.

As the evening's self-appointed master of ceremonies, Laurie directed the guests to the building's two elevators. Daddy bounded for the stairwell. "Mr. Fine, aren't you coming with us?"

"I don't take elewaiters. I take stairs."

"You're going to take the stairs?!" shouted Laurie's girlfriend, her arms filled with balloons. "But it's a long way up!"

"Are you calling me an old man?!" In Daddy's mind, the challenge had been issued. "Just for that, I'm going to take the stairs two at a time!"

Laurie shook his head, smiling at the gang. "Its O.K. We'll meet him in the apartment." Laurie's girlfriend hung back, waiting until an elevator was free. Even alone, almost smothered by balloons, it proved a tight squeeze.

After climbing six flights one stair at a time, Daddy estimated the young people had reached his apartment, so he ducked back into the hallway, hoping he wouldn't run into Laurie's girlfriend. As he sauntered down the corridor to his sixteenth floor apartment Mum stood with her hands on her hips, blocking his path. She was waiting for him, and she was ready. "So where did you wander off to?"

"Nowhere. The elewaiters was full. I took a later elewaiter."

"Sure you did." Ruefully, she shook her head. "Showing off again, eh?" Mum knew her man. She also knew his sweetness. "Darling, you're not 21 anymore." She smiled, in spite of herself. "Now get inside, and act like a host!"

The guests were milling in the apartment. Several of the girls had taken to signing the cast on Mark's foot. Laurie's girlfriend trolled the apartment, rubbing balloons onto the walls until they stuck. Since the guests didn't know where to put their coats and jackets, they kept them on. One glance from Mum was all Daddy needed. He opened the hall closet and began distributing hangers. "Here. Here! Hang youselves up! Make youselves from home!

After greeting Mark, who was sitting on one of Mum's high-backed, petit point chairs like a monarch on a throne, the guests drifted to the dining table and helped themselves to the offerings at the buffet. Daddy had set up a makeshift bar, and appointed himself bartender. "Vot kind wine you want? We have all kinds! We also have cognac!" Daddy poured a dose of the burnt orange brew into a snifter, and presented it to Mark. "For you, *mein* son. You are old enough!"

Marty had recovered from the shock of his first encounter with our dad, and was lounging on the petit pointed, cushioned, and aptly named loveseat. Leslie was in his arms. They were locked in a passionate embrace. Love is said to be blind, and the guests turned a blind eye to the display. Laurie's voice grew strident, and his jokey banter became strained. Mark grew fascinated by a vision on the ceiling visible only to him. I grew intensely uncomfortable. Mum ignored the couple necking in our living room. Daddy did not. He went into the kitchen, removed a pitcher of chilled water from the fridge, opened the freezer and tossed ice cubes into the water, to chill it further, poured out a glassful and nonchalantly strolled behind the loveseat, a devilish gleam glinting in his warm brown eyes. This time, his wife was on the premises. Mum recognized the telltale signs. She launched into alert. "No!" Mum hissed, over the heads of the guests. Desperately she stage-whispered, "Don't you dare!" Daddy hovered over Marty and Leslie while their tongues searched the insides of each other's mouths. The glass in his hand dangled precariously over their heads. Beseechingly, his eyes implored his wife for permission. By her fierce glare he knew permission would not be granted. Dolefully Daddy looked down at the disrespectful couple, then longingly at the glass filled with icy water, in his hand. It was tempting. It was oh so tempting. Valiantly resisting temptation, Daddy lifted the glass to his lips and brushed the back of Marty's head with his elbow, instead. "You two should come up for air," he suggested, strongly, like a doctor. "It's getting hot in here." As Daddy's forearm grazed Marty's head, the younger man noticed the watch on the older man's wrist. It was a cheap watch, the kind worn by workers in his grandfather's factory. Marty sported a Rolex, on his wrist. Like a character out of Oscar Wilde,

176

Schwartz' grandson knew the price of everything, and the value of nothing.

The party proceeded with Daddy's approval. Laughter tinkled, and talk flowed. Gifts were unwrapped, photos were snapped, wineglasses were charged, raised, clinked, and toasts were made. Towards eleven the guests began drifting towards the door. Mark leaned back, like a pasha, on our mother's petit point cushioned armchair. He was slightly tired, and deeply happy. "More apple cake, Ma! And a big, big glass of milk!" Mum and Daddy were seeing the guests out the door.

"I'll get it for you." I went to the dining table and cut my brother a generous slice of his favourite cake.

As soon as the door closed on the last guest Mum's social mask dropped, and she whirled on Daddy. Mum and Daddy adored each other, but they didn't always understand each other. "How could you? How could you?! How could you spoil your son's party in such a way?!"

"I didn't do nuttink!" Daddy protested. Mark and I were blindsided by our mother's sudden attack on our father.

"Oh but you wanted to! You were thinking about it! And you would've done it too, if I hadn't been here to stop you! Your poor son, with his injured foot, and you would've embarrassed him and his friends by pouring cold water over their heads!" Mark smirked. I giggled. Daddy struggled to keep a straight face, which served only to infuriate Mum further. "And what about your daughter?! She worked so hard to create this surprise for her brother, and you almost ruined it!"

I interjected, "But Ma, I don't feel bad."

"You be quiet. I'm talking to your father!"

I sunk back, into myself.

"Honestly Abram! I feel as if I have three children, and

177

you're the biggest baby of them all!" Daddy scratched his head, but the sparkle in his eyes signalled there were still jests left in the court jester.

"Ma, you're blowing this way out of proportion," Mark attempted to defend our dad.

"You go lie down!" Mum brooked no interference. "You need to rest your foot." Mark lifted himself onto his crutches and hobbled off, to his room. Mum shook a fist at her bemused husband. "I know you're laughing inside," she accused, "but you think about what I've said. You need to change your approach! Really Abram, you need to grow up!" Mum stomped off to Mark's room, to tend to her injured boy.

Glumly Daddy shuffled into the dining room. I trailed behind. Cake crumbs dotted the lace-edged tablecloth protecting the dining room table, and broken pieces of cake embedded with baked plums and slivers of apple lay abandoned on bone china dishes. "I'm in the doghouse," Daddy pouted, like a reprimanded child. "She put me in the doghouse." The twinkling lights of the crystal chandelier, like cool candles, were reflected in a darkened window. It was Daddy's gift to Mum, once he could afford to give it to her. I removed the tea and coffee cups. Daddy removed the wine and water glasses and the silverware brought out only for special occasions. He took them to the kitchen and rinsed them in the sink. "We'd better wash these by hand, Daddy. They're delicate, and they might get hurt in the dishwasher."

While I washed dishes, Daddy dampened a small cloth, returned to the dining room, and used the cloth to wipe cake crumbs off the table, allowing them to drop into his free hand. He crossed back into the kitchen and kissed the top of my head, before tossing the crumbs into a plastic-lined garbage can.

"It bugs you, Daddy, doesn't it." Not talking meant

deep thinking. I grew as pensive as my dad.

"Yes, it bugs me. I don't understand how *mein* son is finding such friends."

"I don't get it." I lathered and rinsed the china. Then I handed the dishes, piece by piece, to my dad, who now had a linen towel in his hands. "If strangers come into your house and they almost spoil your party and you want to do something about it, how does Mummy end up making you feel like The Bad Guy?"

"*Och! Mein shepsaleh!*" Daddy carefully dried the china and stacked them, dish by dish, on the kitchen table. "It's because I wanted to do something about it that Mummy made me into The Bad Guy."

"I understand you, Daddy." I picked up a second towel and wiped water droplets off the silver cutlery.

"I know you understand me." Daddy's gaze rested on my profile, as we stood side by side, drying dishes. Tenderly he whispered, "Today is your brother's birthday, and you are the gift."

The party was over. As we tucked away the fancy dinnerware into the drawers of the large credenza Daddy relaxed, knowing he would live on in me.

About the author
S. Nadja Zajdman is a Canadian author. Her short stories have been broadcast on radio, and her short stories and non-fiction pieces have been published in newspapers, magazines and literary journals across North America and in Australia and New Zealand, in publications as diverse as *Chicken Soup for the Soul* and *The Saturday Evening Post*. In 2012 Nadja published her first collection of related short stories: *Bent Branches*, which spans four continents and seventy years in the life of a family. Recently Nadja completed work on a second collection of related short stories as well as a memoir of her mother, the noted Holocaust educator and activist Renata Skotnicka-Zajdman.

The Stuff of Fairytales

L.G. Flannigan

I've been paid a mighty sum to kill her. It would cost the villagers nothing to do it themselves but they are simple god-fearing folk who don't want her blood staining their hands…darkening their souls. Still I'm not complaining as their fear gives me work.

I collect her from the gaol, shackled at the ankles and wrists and wrapped in an oversized cloak. People never cease to surprise me. They want her dead but still they give her protection against the winter cold. A tiny slip of a thing, possibly no more than seventeen winters old, she is easy to bundle in the back of my cart. I make sure her chains are secure so there's no means of escape. She doesn't struggle. How this girl evokes such fear astonishes me. True her kind exist but I refuse to believe that she could tear me to pieces and rip out my heart – that is the stuff of fairytales.

It's usual to provide some proof of death, the body for instance but not this time. Not one single drop of her crimson blood is to return to the village. I'm an honourable man so I'll do as they ask. I will earn the bag of gold that's stowed away in my cart.

As I drive the horse along the track it clears of people, dust flying up as they hurry towards the safety of their homes. Doors bang shut and the scraping and rasping of furniture being pushed up against them echoes out. As we round the corner and disappear from view a breath-like breeze ruffles my hair as if the villagers sigh in collective relief.

I make a stop half way to journey's end and take out my lunch of bread and cheese, kindly prepared by the inn keeper's wife. My captive moves her head a little as if trying to catch a glimpse of what I'm eating. The folds of the cloak mask her face from me. There's little point sharing my food, she'll soon be dead.

The winter sun no longer takes the edge off the cold wind so I eat quickly and move on. It is with some relief I reach the woodland. It gives me some shelter from the bitter wind. Five furlongs in and a path wide enough for my cart splits from the track leading into the deepest part of the wood.

My horse stands stock still his eyes fearful. With a sigh, I get down and take the horse's halter, intent on guiding him but he doesn't budge. Suddenly, he backs away twisting the cart. Holding on tightly I whisper soothing sounds hoping that my cart and its load don't tip over. My stick catches my eye however my horse has fared me well so I won't beat him. Gradually he calms down and I tie him to a tree at the side of the track. It makes sense to proceed on foot.

I take my knife, from the sheath on my belt, and spin it in my hand admiring the blade honed early this morning ready for the deed ahead. It slides easily into its cover – the next time it's in my hand will be to slice open her throat.

Releasing my prisoner from the cart I help her down on to the uneven path and pick up the cloth bag with the remains of my lunch in it and hang it over my shoulder.

Her face is still hidden from my view when I hear her murmur, "You would do well to listen to your stead. It will not be long before the first winter snow falls."

Her voice shocks me; it's of someone older, wiser.

Their words resonate in my ears,

Do not listen to her, do not be fooled.

I heed the villagers' advice. Silently I guide her down the path. Her shackles inhibiting her tread as we move slowly onward.

"Why not kill me here? It is foolhardy to go so far into the woods; the snow will make you lose your way."

"It doesn't snow this far south so early into winter." I

say no more, it doesn't do to entertain the quarry.

"We would make quicker time if you removed my leg irons."

She's right. It'll soon be dark and I'm running out of time. Simpler to kill her here and now but the villagers had been specific.

She must be killed when she's transformed.

It doesn't make sense to me, dead is dead surely, but I'm a man of my word.

With the keys for her shackles back at the gaol I scan the woodland floor picking up a suitable rock. I smash at the chain between her ankles until it gives way.

I grasp the chain that still holds her wrists together and walk on in silence. She easily keeps up with my large strides. The path weaves through the trees and gradually tapers causing me to drop behind her slightly. She looks up.

Out of curiosity I dare to follow her gaze. Through the leafless branches, I see heavy clouds coming in fast covering what is left of the blue sky.

"Hopefully the snow will light our way," she says holding out a shackled, dainty, gloved hand. A single snowflake dances its way down and lands softly on her palm before melting.

I shiver. She's right. It *is* snowing this far south so early into winter.

Stopping we watch as snowflake after fluffy snowflake fall until the path in front and behind us disappears under a blanket of white making me uncertain of the way forward and back. Nothing looks familiar anymore.

As I move forward my boot catches on a root plunging me head first towards a tree trunk.

Gentle breaths caress my face and a tender hand touches my brow. My head is throbbing and my back aches. I'm resting awkwardly against something unforgiving. My heart races, on finding my captive so near.

"You're awake. Good. I was worried," she says.

I'm scared to look at her. There's no clanking of chains as her hands tend to my wound. She is free. Instinctively I check my sheath. Oddly my knife is still there and her cloak covers my legs.

I have to ask, "Why are you helping me?" I try to see her face but chestnut brown ringlets hang down shielding it from me.

She sits back and pushes her hair over her ears. Captivating and beautiful her flawless skin is rosy from the cold. I'm unable to move my eyes from her delicate pink lips as she speaks.

"Because you are hurt."

I allow myself to look into her eyes, just one look. So striking, so large, like sparkling green jewels…so revealing, they hint at what she is. Her long eyelashes flutter as she smiles at me.

"I have cleaned your wound. Thankfully it is not too deep. I think it is wise you rest here for the night as you were out for a while."

Her words mean nothing as I continue to stare.

She turns away shyly.

Her movement breaks my gaze, just in time for I'm so nearly enchanted by her. I shake my head trying to clear it but the dizziness returns. I close my eyes and the spinning stops.

I'm aware of her busying around me.

"Mister?" she whispers.

I force open one eye. "Yes?"

"Do you have any flints in your bag?"

Slowly I sit up. The dizziness has gone and I'm feeling

a bit better. It's stopped snowing. The forest is eerily bright. The moonlight shimmers off the white carpet covering the floor and tree branches. A pile of wood lays outside a circle of stones and some tinder sits at its centre. I take the unopened bag from her and search for my flints.

"You know how to use them?" I ask handing them to her.

She nods. A couple of flashes from the flints and it's not long until a roaring fire keeps the cold away.

"I don't suppose you have any beakers in there?" she says.

"One." *And it's mine.*

Holding out her hand to take it she says, "I'll melt some snow so you can drink."

I watch as she scoops up snow and holds the beaker over the fire.

"You might want to wait until it cools," she says handing it back.

I snatch it off her. She's beginning to irk me. Something's not right. *She is not right.* Any normal person, I use the word loosely, would have stolen my knife, slit my throat and escaped with my horse and cart and yet this thing gives up her cloak for me, cares for me. *What is her angle?*

"What is your name?" she asks poking at the fire.

"How does it help knowing my name?"

"Don't you think I should know the name of my killer? Surely you owe me that."

I suppose she has a point. "William." I say.

"Thank you. Mine is Damsel."

"I don't need to know yours."

Her bottom lip trembles slightly. "I think you should know the name of your quarry."

Hoping to shut her up I say, "And what were the names of yours?"

"I have hurt no one."

I remind myself of their words. *Do not listen to her, do not be fooled.* "That's not what the villagers said."

"They twist the truth to suit their own ends." She twiddles a ringlet round a finger.

It must be the way the fire catches her eyes for they said she is devoid of emotion but yet I see tears. Her clothes are threadbare and without her cloak she has to be cold. *But she has the fire to keep her warm.* I feel her pain for just a second before shutting her out. I can't care about this young woman. I've a job to do.

I take out the remainder of my lunch and begin to eat. Damsel's stomach rumbles noisily. Unable to ignore it I break off a piece of bread and toss it in her direction. Her reflexes are sharp; her hand shoots up catching it. She tucks in hungrily. It makes sense for her to eat if she's to manage the rest of the journey tomorrow.

Finishing off the last of the cheese I ask the question which has been troubling me since I came around. "Why…didn't you…run?" I wipe my mouth with the back of my hand and swallow.

"I am foolish." She gives me a weak smile.

That's no answer. "You'd rather die?"

"No."

"You should have left me."

Damsel puts some more wood on the fire. "We should huddle together for warmth."

It can't hurt. She could've easily killed me by now. I open my cloak and as she slips in beside me I put my arm around her ice cold shoulders pulling her cloak over our legs. Huddled together we have more chance of staving off the cold.

"Thank you," she whispers laying her head on my chest.

I wake only when the sun begins its rise. Damsel is still

asleep and has wrapped herself round my body during the night. She's a little older than I'd first thought and perhaps educated if the way she speaks is anything to go by. It'll be a relief to get this job over with and return to my manor, given to me by a grateful Lord for ridding his land of a bear that had killed his peasants and livestock. It had met my eyes, the hunter now hunted, as I stabbed it through the heart with only a momentary regret for killing such a noble animal. *How will I feel when I slit her throat?*

I try to think of other things. My forehead still hurts and my joints are stiff from the cold. I move a little trying to get comfortable. Her thick cloak, protecting our legs from the worst of the winter, falls to one side. My eyes rest on Damsel again. Her ill-fitting dress exposes a shoulder where many bruises mark her skin from the beating. It's not been the first time either – there are scars too. I sigh heavily trying to dismiss any feelings of sympathy and heed the villagers' warnings. I do laudable work, killing the eviller side of life and her kind *is* the eviller side of life.

My movements disturb her.

Damsel's face reddens as she untangles her legs from mine. She stands up quickly. "Sorry," she mumbles avoiding looking at me. She begins to clear away the remains of last night's one. "I could light another fire and melt some snow so you can have a drink of water."

"No. Best not prolong this." It's my turn to avoid looking at her. Killing her is going to be harder than I expected. Getting up I gather my flints and beaker together and put them in my bag.

"I am a hard worker. I am good at cooking, making fires and caring for people," Damsel blurts out.

Her words hang in the air along with her breath. What is she saying to me? Is she offering herself up as my servant…or maybe more?

"What else are you good at?" I ask eyeing her up and down. Maybe she could satisfy *all* my needs. Her bosom rises and falls anxiously at my scrutiny.

Blushing Damsel looks away. "Nothing else."

Her response irritates me, that she would reject me. "Don't worry, I didn't mean that. I wouldn't touch *you*."

Her shoulders drop. It's as if I've wounded her already. I regret my tone and find myself trying to make amends. "Take the cloak," I say handing it to her.

Gratefully she wraps herself in it and says no more.

Her offer explains why she didn't run when I was unconscious. All alone in the world she seeks company and I'm better than nothing. If I hadn't been paid I might consider it. I sigh. *She should have run when she had the chance.*

We set off down the path. In daylight without snow falling I know the way. Her compliance and silence unnerve me slightly. I find myself uncharacteristically volunteering information.

"It's not much further now." My words fade out towards the end, I'm being tactless. She won't want to know that her death is so very close.

Damsel looks up at me. "I still do not understand why you cannot do it here?"

What harm could it do, she'll know soon enough. "We're heading for a glade, there's a spring which flows strong this time of year."

A single tear runs down her face. She brushes it away and grabs my hands in hers. "Please, do it here."

Her touch sends tingles along my skin. I peel her hands off mine and push her forward. "I'll keep to the original plan."

"But why? Either way I'm dead. And it will probably be frozen. It is much colder than usual. Please." Her voice

187

is high-pitched, desperate.

A little bit of doubt enters my mind. "Possibly."

Her face relaxes a little.

"We'll find out when we get there. As you say, either way you're dead."

Damsel lets out a sob, tears falling down her pale face. "I am begging you, p…please kill me here. I…I cannot go through it again. It hurts and I do not w…want you to see me like that."

I'm unsure whether to comfort her or not, are her words hollow, some part of an elaborate plan to fool me? Whatever the truth is, she's getting to me. I have to hope that she's as terrifying as the villagers say as I might not be able to complete the job if she's a weeping wreck at the water's edge.

I say nothing. The silence is only interrupted by Damsel's decreasing sobs.

"Are you not worried I might hurt you?"

I'm unable to suppress my smile, admiring her trying a different tack.

"No," I reply calmly. *I can't let her mess with my head.*

"Am I not meant to have killed people?"

She is clever, I'll give her that. "Yes, but I'll be strong enough to deal with you and," I deliberately meet her eyes, her glistening, gorgeous sparkling green eyes framed by wet lashes, "I…I know what to expect." *She is the most beautiful woman I've ever seen.*

Her glittering eyes stare pass me and she lets out a cry.

I turn to look. The glade is in view.

Catching me unawares she shouts, "Sorry," and runs back the way we have walked.

Running is futile. I catch up with her in less than seven strides throwing my arms around her body. Our momentum carries us onto the ground, the snow cushioning our fall.

She struggles like a wild cat beneath me.

"You're wasting your time, I'm much stronger than you," I say through gritted teeth. She's proving more troublesome to bring to her feet than I thought she would.

Finally, we're both standing. Damsel has her back pressed into me and my arms are locked firmly around her.

She continues to struggle. "Let me go, let me go!" Her voice is shrill.

"You'll only run away again." *Why is she making this so difficult now?* It won't change anything.

She sinks her teeth into my arm.

"Egad, bitch!" I cry out, pushing her to the ground.

Damsel leaps to her feet set to run again but this time I'm ready for her seizing one of her arms and swinging her round to face me. With my free hand, I deal a resounding slap to her face. She cowers away from me. I don't make a habit of hitting women but an eye for an eye and all that.

Holding on tightly to her wrist I expect her to struggle but all her fight has gone. She walks meekly, head down, into the glade.

It's usually a place I visit in the summer months when I've a maiden to entertain. Covered in a layer of virgin snow the glade looks magical. The gushing spring is reduced to a gentle trickle as some of its flow hangs from the rocks like ice daggers. I lead her over to the pool and pick up a broken branch using it to crack through the thin layer of ice that covers the surface. The water will be freezing. *Can I really do this to her?*

"Please kill me here. William, please, it will be too cold."

The way she says my name makes me falter. But I couldn't kill her like she is; she poses no threat to me, to anyone, like this. She has to transform, it'll be easier to dispose of her once she's less than human.

I let go of her wrist and undo the ties of her cloak. My fingers touch her neck and I notice her swallow, my eyes meet hers. Forcing myself to look away I watch her cloak fall to the ground.

Next I remove the cord wrapped around her waist.

A tear tracks slowly down her cheek. "I will take it off," she says in a hoarse whisper. She pulls the shapeless grey cloth dress over her head revealing an off-white fitted bodice and underskirt.

The sight of Damsel is captivating. I drink in her every curve, every contour. I battle the urge to remove all her clothing.

She bites her bottom lip and takes a step away from me. She's seen the lust in my eyes. A more experienced woman would offer herself to me, would use her wiles to bargain her way out but not this little thing. I feel sorry for her. Struggling to bring myself back to the task I try to remind myself what the villagers said – *she needs to be fully submerged.*

I pull back my shoulders and take a calming breath before guiding her to the pool's edge.

"Take off your boots," I say attempting to take control of the situation and my emotions.

Damsel does as she's told.

I give her a gentle push in her back.

She dips one foot in the water, gasping she pulls it out.

"Keep going." I make my voice as gruff as possible.

The pool is deep and Damsel is up to her shoulders within two steps. I lean over and put my hand on her head and push her under. She thrashes her arms wildly but I don't let her up until I'm satisfied it's been long enough.

She emerges spluttering and gasping for air. Her hair is plastered to her face and her teeth chatter together noisily. I help her out of the water. Her undergarments cling to her body revealing her naked form, her nipples erect.

She moans, "Let go of me, please."

I can't, not when she looks like that. I regret pushing her in. I should have taken her home, to look after her and love her.

Stronger than before she shakes off my grip and falls to the ground on all fours letting out a shrill scream. Her face is contorted in pain.

I take a step back.

Her back arches and she grasps at the snow sobbing. "Go away!" she shrieks.

"I don't fear you." I pick up her cloak and rush to wrap it around her, to stop her shivering.

She throws off the cloak. "I don't w...want you to watch."

Her eyes plead with me. There's not only pain but shame in them, hatred of what she's about to become, of what I'll see. Compelled to watch I can't obey her.

She throws back her head and screams in agony. Through her sobs, I hear the terrifying splitting of skin. Her finger nails tear open her gloves growing into sharp claws. Blood seeps through the back of her bodice and drop by drop falls onto the snow. The cloth on her back rips apart. A pair of iridescent wings breaks through quickly followed by a second pair. They're beautiful, mesmerizing colours of turquoise and purple.

Damsel's sobs evaporate. I watch fascinated as she stretches out her limbs like an animal no longer trapped and spreads out her wings; they glisten in the low winter sun. A faint smile glimmers across her face and she sighs contentedly.

Reluctantly I reach for my knife. My hand hovers over its sheath all the while looking, not wanting to take my eyes off her.

191

Her lashes slowly flutter over her seemly larger eyes as if she's adjusting to their new size. They're a shimmering green and it's as if they've cast a spell on me as I'm unable to move, to complete my task.

A robin flies in front of me and lands on a low hanging branch; it puffs out its chest and chirrups catching Damsel's attention. Slowly she licks her lips – *she has never looked more beautiful* – her long supple tongue flicks out seizing the bird and whipping it into her mouth. She crunches on the poor defenceless animal.

My stomach churns. Maybe the villagers were right, her kind tore people apart but I'm still not so sure *she* will. The image of the poor defenceless girl clashes wildly with the creature before me.

I've given my word, accepted their gold, it'll only take me three strides to reach her and slit her throat. I draw my knife from its sheath and take a step towards her; the sun's rays catch the blade, the glare flashing across her face.

She turns her head towards me opening her mouth to reveal rows of razor sharp teeth. They're dripping with blood and feathers.

I've lost my moment to strike.

She flicks her wings and hovers slightly above the snow inching little by little towards me.

I take a stumbling step back and fall onto the ground dropping my knife. She flitters over me moving her head from side to side studying every bit of my body. She's so close her breath ruffles my hair. I can see every single one of her razor-sharp teeth. *Is this to be the last few seconds of my life?*

She reaches out a clawed finger and runs it down the side of my face. Perhaps she is trying to be careful but nevertheless she draws blood.

It oozes a warm path down my neck.

Humming to herself she pulls back her finger and licks it lovingly, a drop of saliva hitting my nose.

I look into her sparkling black eyes and Damsel is no longer there. A darker being stares hungrily back at me. With it so close I am pinned down with no way of escaping. Blindly my fingers grapple in the snow for my lost knife, bile rising in my throat.

The winged being tilts its head as if listening to my erratic breathing, its eyes concentrating on my heaving chest.

Its claws make easy work of my clothes, the tips shredding through the first layer of my skin. If I'm to have my heart ripped out I pray it'll be quick. My world starts to spin.

"Damsel!" I cry out in one last desperate attempt for her to return.

Startled, it pulls back allowing me a little breathing space. The darkness has gone, her eyes return to a shimmering green and swim with tears as she studies my wounds. She opens her mouth and lets out a long piercing scream. Without warning she takes off vertically into the sky and is gone.

I lie on the freezing snow staring up through the trees for some glimpse of her. I'm torn between relief and regret that she's gone. Aching from the cold and bleeding from my chest I sit up. Thankfully the wounds aren't too deep.

Damsel's pile of belongings lay abandoned next to me. I collect her damp cloak, boots and dress and put them in my bag along with my knife before making my way back down the path.

For the first time in my life I've reneged on a deal, failed at my job. I'm unsure what to do. *Return the gold?* It would only frighten the villagers and Damsel is unlikely to return there.

She needs someone looking after her. Not a man taking her to spring water, forcing her to transform, forcing her to be evil. *I've been a fool.*

I throw my bag in the back of my cart and untie my horse. Out of the corner of my eye there's a fleeting movement in the shadows. My heart leaps, sitting in the cart is Damsel tear-stained, her hair hanging in rats' tails and her undergarments in a shocking bloody state.

"Sorry," she mouths. Her eyes fall on the empty sheath hanging from my belt.

I give a little smile and walk over to the back of the cart. I rummage through the bag and pull out her clothes. I help her put on the dress, tie up her boots and drape the cloak over her shoulders.

"Thank you." Sighing, she parts my cloak and shredded clothes with her bloodied fingers and stares at my bloody chest, "I should clean you up."

"It'll wait 'til we get home," I say grabbing the reins and climbing up to sit beside the girl who has captured my heart but so very nearly ate it.

About the author

L.G. Flannigan loves dark chocolate and her children, husband and dog. She lives in Somerset and, when not writing, works in a library. She writes contemporary adult and young adult novels plus the occasional short story. having been published in the *On This Day*, *Snowflakes* and *Baubles* anthologies. Her contemporary novel *Ordering Flynn Matthews*, shortlisted in Choc-Lit's Search for a Star Competition, was published in July 2016. The follow-on novel, *Failing Flynn Matthews*, was published in August 2017. L.G.'s musings can be found at http://lgflannigan.com.

To Wish Upon a Star

Paula R C Readman

As the inky purple sky began to lighten, luminous arcs of brilliant blue and yellow flashed diagonally towards the horizon. In the distance against the retreating darkness, the mountain tops shimmered with a halo of silvery gold light as day forcefully regained its place once more.

Estella, with a heavy heart, stepped away from the reinforced glass window. Maybe she had been too hasty waiting all night, but she felt she couldn't afford to miss the opportunity to win her heart's desire, if the legend was true.

Swinging the weighty protective curtain aside, it caught her delicate lace robe, pulling it from her porcelain shoulders. As the curtain fell back into place, it blocked out the growing heat from the morning light. She wondered if the forces would be stronger tonight as it was the beginning of the Belili Festival.

The festival celebrated the return of the first spring moon as it rose over the planet of Beltane. With its return came the first meteor shower of the season so she was reassured that she would certainly get her wish granted.

As she crossed the stone-tiled floor, the only sound that echoed within the viewing tower in the granite castle that she called home was her bare feet as she headed for the stairs. Shivering slightly, Estella pulled her robe back up and tightened the belt again. She wasn't aware of the cold as she descended into the living quarters buried deep underground.

Reaching the corridor that led to the bedrooms, she paused briefly before the solid fireproof door. Her hesitation took her by surprise for a second, but as the tension dispersed and she relaxed, her mind began processing the key numbers she needed to enter.

"Remember," she said reassuring herself as she tapped on the keypad. "This is still all relatively new to you."

As the door slid open and she stepped forward, a picture of Hyman, her life's partner flashed across her mind. She recalled the vivid image of him as he lay sleeping last night. He lay on his side covered only by a finely woven silk sheet, as he drifted off to sleep, his breathing soft and steady, his left arm slipped off the side of the bed.

During the night, she'd lain awake listening as he drifted into a deeper sleep, it was easier for her to slip from his side. Unable to sleep herself, her thoughts began to replay the scenes featured in the archive videos especially the ones containing groups of people known as *'families'*.

The discovery of such things had confused her, even more so was the fact the units known as the *'family'* were made up of a man known as a *father*, and a woman known as a *mother*, thus creating her obsession *'with child'*.

At first, she hadn't grasped the full meaning, not fully understanding how to unlock the secret of creation, she'd hunted through hours of footage. The only reference she found of interest led her to believe that the mothers carried their child within them.

All she really did understand was the growing need within her to create a smaller version of Hyman and herself. She wondered whether the men and women on the screen had created their *children* in a similar sort of way as Hyman had created their home, carving it out of living rock.

After the fire door buzzed open, it softly closed behind her, she hesitated again.

"If I tried to return to Hyman's side, my coldness will wake him and then he'll ask me where I've been. No, it's much better for him to find me in the bathing room, should he wake and find me gone."

She crossed to the door opposite, and entered. After hanging her robe on a hook, she released the array of grips that held her soft angel blonde hair in a topknot before entering the misting cubicle. As she waited while a light scanned her body to calculate the amount of water needed, her mind filled with thoughts about the shooting stars, recalling how she had come across the legend while searching the archives.

Once the misting light finished tiny jets of warm water began spraying her from above and from the sides of the cubicle. Turning slowly to allow the mist to dampen her body and hair, Estella pondered on the details of the shooting star legend, wondering why it didn't give a full explanation.

The missing data she wanted she knew would help to empower her wish, but so far she hadn't been able to clarify whether it was the first shooting star she saw, or the very first one of the season that she needed to wish upon. All she really knew about the shooting stars were they came in twofold, first at the beginning of the year, known as Candlemas and then again at the year's end, the winter solstice. Unable to ask Hyman about the legend meant she needed to take a gamble, but logic told her that the power of the wish would be greater at the beginning of the season, rather than the end.

Once the misting cubicle had completed its first cycle, a blue hue emanated from above, and travelled down the full length of her body. While she waited for it to finish, her mind went back to the legend.

She couldn't understand the logic of it. According to the data she'd read at the beginning of the spring festival, if you wished upon the first bright shooting star of the season it would grant your heart's desire. However, by the end of the year, the same legend also foretold that the inhabitants of the planet needed to offer prayers to their many Gods to help them survive the long, cold winter months.

"Why only one wish," she muttered turning around in the blue light. "It makes me feel as though I'm putting my wants and needs, above that of the whole community."

After cleansing her body of any harmful bacteria, the programme moved onto its rinsing cycle. As Estella turned slowly in the mist, she ran her hands over her fine curves and full, soft breasts, trying to imagine what changes would happen to it if she were to be with child.

Finally, the misting cubicle filled with warm air to dry off her body and hair.

"How wonderful, it will be when we are a family," she muttered stepping out and gathering up her robe, and dropped it into a washer.

Pulling on her cream linen dress, she re-pinned her hair, her mind still on the legend. There were many questions she needed answered, questions about creation. She knew Hyman and the other miners understood the geological structure of the planet, but what about the creation of life?

Letting out a soft sigh, she checked herself in the mirror, her bright, questioning green eyes sparkling back at her.

"I shall just have to solve the mystery on my own," she told her reflection. "Hyman would just laugh at me for indulging in such primitive nonsense."

Arriving only six months ago, Estella found living on a desolate planet left her experiencing despondence. However, the beauty of her new home ignited her curiosity, with its clean lines, and natural features. The black granite towers of castle-like buildings that dotted the surface sparkled in the burning light of the planet's two suns. Hyman, a mining engineer and designer, explained that the towers were where the miners lived but had a second important job. Firstly, they were oxygen-pumping towers that allowed the men to move freely below, as well as vents to release the build-up of heat from the mines deep within the bowels of the planet.

She clearly remembered being in awe of the tall, iron-muscular man, dressed in light brown cotton trousers and a plain white tunic. Unlike the striking surroundings, he had a realistic quality about him that won her heart. She couldn't take her eyes off his chiselled features, the soft lines around his azure eyes, and his solid lips. When he spoke the sound of his firm, but steady voice left her speechless. She drank in Hyman's excitement as he guided her around her new home. As she followed in his wake, he led her from room to room, explaining as they went the idea behind having the living quarters built deep within the bedrock of the planet.

"By centralising the main living space and having all the other rooms leading off from it by a series of easy to operate air and fire doors, I was able to construct the viewing towers and utility rooms as separate entities from the main body of the castle.

"This not only allows us to keep our living quarters at a steady temperature but much cooler than the outside world. It also keeps us safe and gives us more freedom to move around without cumbersome oxygen tanks and heat protective clothing," Hyman said, proudly, while watching her reactions carefully, she thought. "The harsh reality of the outer landscape makes this planet, one of the most difficult to inhabit." He continued with a sweeping gesture of his hand to the room. "With that in mind, I wanted each of the rooms to reflect a perfect sense of balance. By harmonizing the colour scheme of pale greens, blues, and yellows, hopefully it will give its inhabitants a sense of security while being at one with the natural world outside."

Suddenly aware he had finished speaking she turned to study his face. As his eyes brightened, the lines around them and his lips became more defined as his smile illuminated his countenance. She felt a strange warming sensation that caressed her cheeks, making her lower her eyes.

"Good," he said.

She waited for him to enlighten her to why she was good, but instead he just nodded. She wondered if he was expecting her to ask some questions, but she couldn't think of any.

Aware of unease within the silence that lingered between them she longed to hear his voice, for him to continue explaining the aspects of her new home, and her role within it, but he said nothing.

She waited conscious only of her thoughts.

After a moment, he slipped his hand into hers. His grip was strong yet gentle, even though his hands were rough to her touch. Now he guided her with his arm around her waist as they continued the tour of the house. They climbed a wide stone staircase and stopped before a curtained panoramic window.

She registered the deepening tone of his voice as he emphasised the seriousness of what he was saying. "As beautiful as the view maybe, my dear, it's very important that these curtains are kept in place at all times. They are sensitive to heat and light and are here to protect us."

He pointed beyond them and across the wide balcony towards the huge domed spheres that rose into the night sky. Like Hyman, the other wealthy miners had chosen to build their granite castles facing the domed gardens of sheer wonder, an oasis of flowing water, plants, and trees.

"The gardens," he explained, "are not just things of

beauty, but help to sustain life on this difficult, but wealthy planet. We have succeeded where others have failed, by bringing with us wildlife that has flourished. Thus supplying us with fresh food, which the early explorers could only dream of when they came to colonise the planets within Delta-V

As he spoke the shimmering mountain and the clear sparkling sky drew Estella's attention. Like dazzling jewels, their brightness would have blinded anyone who didn't have a curtain or light sensitive reinforced glass to protect them.

As they made their way back downstairs, he continued explaining the many features of her new home,

"The lighting throughout the house is set to coincide with the changing artificial seasons outside. It also helps to keep our body clock in check, making sure we get enough sleep. The early settlers decided the best hope for survival here was to be in tune with the planet itself."

"I understand," she said, smiling at him.

"That's very good." He returned her smile, which pleased her, and then continued; "I know this is all new to you, Estella. I'm sure you will soon feel at home here with me. Come let me show you the kitchen."

For the first three months, she found her routine pleasurable. After sharing breakfast with her, Hyman left for work. Her chores were simple enough, making sure his clothes were ready for the next day, the house clean, and meals prepared, ready for his homecoming. Working in a hot atmosphere, the miners sweated pints, so they changed clothes every hour throughout their long working day, arriving home shattered, grimy, and hungry.

One evening, Estella found herself becoming a little

impatient with Hyman. He had finished work later than usual. While she waited for him to shower, and slip into something more comfortable, ready to dine, she paced the floor. Everything had been prepared on time. She'd already set up the dining table and transported their meal upstairs into the viewing tower, before he'd come home.

Throughout the meal, she found their conversations laboured. Unable to think of anything more to say she'd given up. By the time, she began to clear the table; she could no longer contain her disappointment. She understood he was tired, but she'd waited patiently for his stimulating conversation as she had nothing else to fill her long, uneventful day.

Laying down his cutlery it seemed to her that Hyman was ignoring her as he reached for his iPad. Estella felt her isolation take on a physical form as she finished her chores, and took her place beside him to wait for the two suns to set over the mountains marking the end of another dissatisfying day for her.

Hyman lowered his iPad, his questioning eyes searching her face as he asked, "What's wrong, my dear?"

Taken aback by the tone of his voice she said nervously, "Is this all there is to my life? Just cleaning, cooking, and sharing recipes, new cleaning ideas, and small talk with the other women while you chatter about more interesting things with the other miners. I find women's things inferior."

He smiled at her.

"Is it so wrong of me to say so?"

"Not at all, my dear, I'm so pleased you want to expand your mind. Come, come."

Standing he took her soft hand in his and led her downstairs to a solid reinforced door she hadn't noticed before. After pressing his finger to a small pad, the door slid open. She followed him in and stood staring in wonder at a large screen.

"Everything you need to know about the history of this planet and more are in these," he said, pulling a disc from its case and slipping it into a slot before tapping the screen.

She stood in awe as groups of people appeared before her. A light informative voice began to explain how the first men had arrived to extract the planet's vast rich deposits of minerals and precious metals.

Estella clapped her hands together in excitement as Hyman pulled her to him kissing the top of her head.

"Now my dear," he said, "I shall programme the door so you can open it but you must only come here while I'm at work, and I expect all your other household chores to be done."

Now their mealtimes became the highlight of her day as the conversation flowed more freely. She enjoyed his praise and laughter as she chatted excitedly about all the new discoveries learnt from the library.

"My sweet darling, Estella," he said, kissing her lightly on the brow while brushing her hair back from her dark green eyes. "What silly things you're filling your head with, but I'm glad you're enjoying learning for yourself."

"They aren't silly things." She pushed him playfully away. "Do you not ever wonder what life is like back on the Mother Planet where the sky was once a softer, gentler blue and everywhere was green?"

She felt Hyman tense as he rose and crossed to the window. Pushing the curtain aside, he placed his hands on the glass. She saw the penetrating heat register on his face, recalling too, the painful sadness within his eyes as his image reflected back at her from the glass.

Aware all too soon the heat of the day would be

completely gone, she knew their time in the tower was nearly over as the chilling, killing cold of the night would soon drive them below again.

"Earth." That's what it was called, Estella, Mother Earth," he said, tears trickling down his cheeks.

"Do you remember it?"

"No, I'm far too young. Only the stories of its existence," he said, brushing at his face with his fingertips.

"It must have been a wonderful place," she said dreamily. "Can you imagine walking about outside in air you can breathe freely while listening to birds' song and picking wild flowers."

He turned to her, and she noticed that lights across the colony were slowly going out behind him.

"Yes, I've often wondered what it must have been like to enjoy such freedom from fear, but still we have a wonderful, but restricted life here. Come, my love," he whispered softly, reaching for her hand. "It's time to sleep." Kissing the back of her hand, he led her down to their bedroom.

Standing before her, he slipped the loosely fitted gown from her shoulders, and it pooled at her feet. Then one at a time, he removed the grips from her hair, and with his fingertips, he brushed it out before kissing the top of her shoulders. Then in one effortless sweep of his arms he scooped her up and laid her gently down on the bed, before climbing in beside her.

Estella hoped tonight would be the night when his kisses revealed his passion for her, but instead, he gently brushed her cheek, told her how beautiful she was before hugging her to him as sleep overpowered him.

Her mind began to recite words of love and romance she'd discovered while reading references books. Was it possible, she wondered if she shared those words of love with him that somehow it might release his passion for her, and trigger the creation of a child, she longed for?

Her mind raced with a question that had been bothering her: just why weren't there any children within the colony?

Why weren't there?

She'd wanted to ask Hyman, but after his comment about her thoughts being *silly things*, she was reluctant to do so. At the monthly meeting with the other miners, she'd questioned the women, but like her, they knew nothing about children.

When she'd tried to explain what she understood about them the women just laughed at her, saying, "Children indeed. We have enough to do with cooking, cleaning, and seeing to our men's needs to worry about such things."

As she laid in the darkness waiting for Hyman to slip peacefully into a deeper sleep after a long busy day, she placed her hand on her perfectly flat stomach, and chanted her longing into the darkness.

Tomorrow marked the beginning of the Belili Festival, when the goddess of trees, love, and the underworld returned. Estella hoped it would mark the beginning of her first full year of discoveries, and hopefully a child that she could share her knowledge with too.

Just at that moment, in sleep Hyman's breathing altered, and he rolled away from her. Turning her head slightly, she checked the clock; just another hour to go. Her thoughts shifted to when she found the entry in an e-book on mythology of shooting stars and wishes; the revelation had at last given her the information she had sought.

As Hyman's breathing slowed to a steady pace, Estella briefly wondered whether the other women were right.

Why couldn't she be as contented as they were? After all, they had only been on the planet for the same amount of time as she, yet what had triggered this growing need within her?

Her normal routine allowed her to slip out of the bed long before Hyman woke, but still she was always cautious not to disturb him. Stepping away from the bed, she unconsciously turned to admire her life's partner.

Hyman lay on his side. Beneath the sheet, highlighted by the growing shimmering light in the room the fine details of his sculptured, muscular body stood out clearly for her to enjoy.

She studied his face. Below his eyelids she saw his eyes move rapidly in sleep, and wondered if he dreamt about the same things as she did: to have a child in their image. Automatically, she reached out to brush the strands of his long, dark, brown hair away from his strong shoulders. His face, handsome with full, kissable lips, and high-bridged nose gave it an air of dignity as familiar to her as her own face was, she thought, catching a shadowy glimpse of herself in the mirror over the bed.

Smiling she recalled their first encounter six months ago, glad he'd chosen her to share his life's journey. Highly respected in their community, Hyman she'd learnt was a kind, thoughtful man in all aspects of their shared life, but she couldn't understand why he didn't display the passion spoken of in poetry and novels from the old world. As the lights began to flicker, she knew the time for wishing had arrived and headed for the door.

Suddenly as though Hyman sensed her thoughts, he rolled on to his back. She froze, fearing he would wake. If he woke now, her opportunity would be gone, knowing he would question her sanity. After all, a man of science

206

wouldn't hold with making wishes on falling pieces of long dead planets, but she had no other choice.

Not knowing whether her wish would be more potent made inside, or outside of the castle, Estella stepped out onto the balcony. The air buzzed with electricity and tingled against her skin. Ignoring the dryness in her nostrils and throat, she lifted her arms to the heavens and focused on how pure the stars looked against the inky black sky high above her.

Taking a few steps forward, she felt her fine lace gown lift from her body as a surprisingly warm light breeze raced across her skin like a lover's touch. She let out a soft sweet moan of pleasure as the first shower of fast moving meteors lit up the night sky with brilliant flashes. As her mind acknowledged the good fortune such a magnificent display of shooting stars would bring the colony, a pounding noise behind her broke the silence.

Glancing over her shoulder, she saw Hyman banging on the reinforced glass. Estella registered that he was gesturing to her, but his words were lost as she felt the powerful warmth race up her naked body and through her blond hair. As her eyes closed against the brightness of the glowing embers, she felt nothing more.

Hyman rested his forehead against the hot glass momentarily as his arm dropped to his side. Stepping back, he allowed the heavy protective curtain to drop back into place, blocking out the view as the cosmic storm snatched away the pile of glittering ash on the other side of the glass.

He shook his head slowly, letting out a long sigh, as he muttered softly, "Not again. Why on earth do they keep doing that to themselves?"

As the swirling dust carried away the fading image of Estella's beauty, Hyman wondered for the third time what it was he was doing wrong. He took no pleasure in watching all his hard work going to waste again. "Perhaps, I'm being a little overzealous with the programming, making my Life Partner Android too realistic by adding all those little extras like free-thought and retaining information."

Making his way down to his laboratory, he began questioning his desire to have a precise copy of his beautiful wife, Estella, to comfort him through their long separations.

"Oh well, it'll keep me busy for the next six months while building another replacement. By the time the meteor storm has finished, I'll be able to meet up with the other guys to see how they're coping with their L.P.As," he muttered as the lab door closed behind him.

About the author

Paula lives in Essex, with husband, Russell, and a cat who adopted them called 'Willow'. In 2010 she had her first success when English Heritage published her story in *Whitby Abbey – Pure Inspiration*. Since then she has won two writing competitions, including having a story selected as the overall winner by best-selling crime writer, Mark Billingham, and had several other short stories published too.

Find out more about Paula and her writing on her Amazon Author page and on her blog:
http://paulareadman1wordpress.com.

Whispers

Julie Swan

She had been sure that the house had whispered to her. *You should live here. Buy me. Buy me.*

Ellie sighed as she looked out at the view. It certainly was a wonderful view. She wished she had someone to share it with. Not just anyone, of course. It had to be someone special, someone companionable to remark on the different types of vessel making their way along the Channel, to speculate where they had come from or where they were going. Someone to be comfortable with.

A guardian angel must have been guiding her when she'd found the cottage. She'd been idly perusing property websites on the internet, mainly trying to find a value for her own property, when something inspired her to enter the search parameters for something with a sea view in the price range she was prepared to pay. She didn't care where it was but she'd hankered after a home by the sea since she'd been a child.

She'd been determined to move. Since she worked from home, location didn't really matter, although the southern part of England was surely to be favoured over the northern part of Scotland. Not because Scotland wasn't beautiful but being within easy reach of London was preferable. There was the odd circumstance when face-to-face meetings were inevitable for her work, there were occasional special deliveries to be made and there were the theatres, museums and galleries which she didn't want to do without.

And when she was ready, she had a lot of friends in London. They would probably visit her on the south coast but not in the wilds of Scotland.

So, much as she liked the cabin on the loch and the croft by the sea she'd made a short list of properties on the south coast. And it had been a short list. She would get much more for her money as she travelled north.

The list comprised a tiny fisherman's cottage in Cornwall, a town flat in Dorset – with marvellous views over Poole harbour it must be admitted – and a small dilapidated three-bedroomed cottage in West Sussex. They all had sea views. She tried to find each of them on Google Earth and found the Cornish and Dorset offerings but, although she could find the Sussex cottage on the aerial views it couldn't be seen on street view as it was hidden away from any made-up road, a distinct point in its favour.

She contacted the agent and arranged to view it. The agent seemed embarrassed at having to show such a run-down property and tried to be upbeat. "Parts of the cottage date back to the early 18th century. There's a lot of history here." He mentioned that it would probably soon be snapped up by a developer who would knock it down and build something more modern. *No, no, no.* He also mentioned something else.

"A famous artist lived here once."

"Really?"

"Yes, some chap called Jack Stabb, back in the thirties. Very famous he was, tremendous artist evidently, but died young."

Ellie said nothing. The agent started making suggestions; a conservatory here, a patio there, central heating, perhaps even an extension.

But there'd been no need for arm-twisting. Ellie had fallen in love with it as soon as she saw it despite the rotting windows and peeling paintwork. Even the dirt of several years and ivy encroaching into the bedrooms didn't put her off. The bay windows at the front overlooking the sea and the privacy afforded by being away from civilisation down a track from the road made it perfect.

There was a back bedroom with a large window facing north that would make a wonderful studio; perhaps it had been Jack Stabb's. There was a small and filthy but seemingly serviceable bathroom. Outside there was a separate garage and a large outhouse both of which appeared to be weather-proof. There was even a rough path down the small cliff to the beach, which was barely accessible any other way and therefore practically private.

It was within walking distance of a village with basic facilities, should she need them, and within a fifteen minute drive of larger towns. She'd found the drive down from London perfectly manageable and it was even fairly close to a main rail line.

But at the cottage, it was so peaceful it could have been the only building in the world. And it had whispered to her.

The one blessing – if it could be thought of as such a thing – was that the insurance on Alex's life and the sale of their two-bedroomed flat in Chiswick would give her enough to buy the cottage outright and still have funds to fall back on. They would probably be needed to make it habitable.

To the agent's great surprise, she immediately offered the asking price and queried if she could get some work done on the house before completion. "I'd like to move in as soon as possible," she told him.

"I don't see any problem with that," the agent said. "I ought to check but the owners aren't really interested. It's taken them years to put it up for sale. It'll be at your own risk, of course, just in case the deal falls through."

Ellie had been happy with that arrangement and had

211

spent the next four weeks 'camping out', cleaning, stripping back the ivy and generally making the place habitable. She organised getting the floorboards sanded and varnished, and then whitewashed all the walls.

She arranged for a local gardener to tame the overgrown plot. He did a good job, taming the vegetable garden and even finding an old cobbled patio under years of wilderness.

A telephone line and broadband were installed so she could contact her agent. A whole day was spent with a mild-mannered middle-aged man from the Fuel Advisory Board discussing the state of the chimneys, wood-burning stoves and, most importantly, how to keep the range (which provided all her hot water) going. No conservatories, no extensions. Major changes, if she decided she wanted them, could wait. For the moment, the peacefulness and the view of the ever-changing sea were enough.

Occasionally as she worked, she thought she heard more whispers. *You're doing the right thing. You will love living here. You belong here.* But she was never sure it wasn't just her imagination.

As soon as the cottage was officially hers, she moved in despite still having to 'camp out'.

Then she went looking for furniture and gradually it became a home. Nothing too elaborate. Most of the modern things in the flat wouldn't have fitted the cottage either size-wise or aesthetically. She included most of it in the sale, bringing only the contents of her studio and a few odd favourite pieces. She scoured junk shops, salvage yards and auction houses finding beds (buying new mattresses of course), tables, chairs, a dresser, odd bits to hold her clothes and knick-knacks; not heavy mahogany pieces but things in lighter woods. Nothing matched but when put altogether it made a pleasing whole. She bought bright new cushions, rugs and throws which brought some cheer, some happiness, into the rooms. *That's nice.*

She'd been here for three weeks now. She'd set up her studio in the north-facing bedroom and had started to think about work again. Her agent, Suzie, had been very patient after Alex's sudden death. As an illustrator of children's stories, she'd been half way through a couple of books when her world had fallen apart. One had been given to another artist but Suzie had put the second on hold until Ellie felt able to continue. "It's just your sort of thing," she said. "All fairies and magic. No-one can do that sort of thing better than you." Ellie was very grateful and had started on a few new sketches for approval.

But the view was such a draw. She'd make herself a mug of tea, sit in the seat in the bay window and watch and listen to the sea. She'd be there for hours.

Never the same, is it?

"No," she murmured.

It took her some minutes to realise that she'd answered the whisper. Was she going mad? Houses didn't whisper in her experience – or anybody's. Was the cottage haunted? Did it matter? She felt very at home there. If there were residing spirits they must be well-meaning.

She began to think of all the people who'd lived in the house before her. She knew about the previous owner, an elderly lady who'd died, fortunately in a nursing home and not in the house. Although some other previous occupants may have. In fact, considering the age of the cottage it was more than likely. If the estate agent was to be believed at least one of them had been quite famous although most of them probably were not. Normal people. They'd lived, loved and finally left one way or another. You couldn't see them, you couldn't hear them – usually – but perhaps they were still around.

213

Was that whisper real or was she losing it?

She decided to google Jack Stabb and found that there had been an artist with that name based in West Sussex in the thirties. Wikipedia told her that he'd moved there after his wife had died in childbirth in her early twenties and that he'd become very reclusive. His paintings had been well received and he'd exhibited in the Royal Academy. He'd died in his late forties and therefore his body of work was quite small. They fetched high amounts on the rare occasion they came up for sale. There were no pictures of him. 'Jack Stabb shunned publicity,' the article said, 'and no images of him are available.'

There were a few examples of his work, mainly seascapes. They had a depth that drew her in and she enlarged the pictures as much as she could on her mega-sized desktop screen to study the technique, zooming in here and there to try and see the actual brushstrokes. However, she knew that, competent illustrator that she was, she wasn't an artist. She could never match the vibrancy and movement that he had portrayed.

How tragic, to lose your wife under such circumstances. 'He came here for much the same reasons as I did,' she thought to herself. For peace and healing.

She felt the cottage surrounding her, almost hugging her, like an old thick winter coat, protecting her against cold reality. If there actually was a presence, it was definitely a friendly one.

She gradually settled into a routine of shopping, housework and occasional gardening in the mornings which gave her the afternoons to think about her work. Ellie's favourite method was to paint the pictures and then scan them into her computer, although some commissions required other techniques. Occasionally the original paintings were sold to advertise the books.

She was working on a picture of fairies flitting between flowers. *How about a little pale lemon just there for highlights?* Obviously there was no pointing finger but she knew just where he meant.

She tried it. It looked much better. *Nice. Maybe a touch of green here, viridian or slightly darker, just to give it some more depth.* That worked too. She went over the whole picture employing the same techniques. When she'd finished she stood back and scrutinised it. It was one of the best illustrations she'd ever done.

Her commission was for a 16-page book but she had already agreed the basic format with Suzie and the author and had sketches of where her drawings were required. She just needed to produce the pictures. She went back and looked at the couple she'd already done for this particular book. Perhaps a little pale lemon and a touch of dark green would help these too. She tried it – and it worked.

I think a hint of vermilion would go well just there. It finished things off beautifully.

The advice didn't come every time she worked. Sometimes there'd be nothing for days but, usually as she was completing a picture, there'd be little whispers of a highlight here, a lowlight there. And it always seemed to make her pictures better.

There was nothing sinister about it, it was just gentle tutelage. No repercussions if she didn't take the advice, although she invariably did. Sometimes a suggestion didn't work and Ellie would paint it out again. *I'm not always right. You must always be prepared to experiment.* It helped to have an objective view.

She worked steadily for weeks until all the required illustrations were completed to her – and the house's (Jack's?) – satisfaction. She scanned them and sent them to Suzie.

Suzie was on SKYPE within the hour, enthusing wildly. "These are marvellous. Even better than your usual work. Well done Ellie. The author's going to love them. I think we'll have a hit on our hands." Ellie could almost hear the unspoken 'Losing Alex was awful but it's made you a better artist,' but thankfully Suzie didn't say it.

"I've got a couple more story books for you," Suzie told her. "I'll send down the details. See what you think."

Once again Ellie was sitting on the window seat with a mug of tea watching the sea.

Wonderful view isn't it? You should paint it.

"No, I'm not good enough," Ellie murmured.

I'll help. It was enough encouragement to try.

Look at that yacht keeling over. Fix it in your mind's eye. You could take a photo but that won't give you the movement. You have to remember the wind, the spume, the colour of the sea and the sky. You have to remember the light. You have to live and breathe it.

Ellie produced a painting she never thought herself capable of. It had life, movement, the colours blended beautifully.

That fishing boat is interesting. Lots of industry there. Great composition. Try and get a quick sketch.

The first few efforts were good but, in Ellie's view, only acceptable amateur paintings. She might get a few hundred pounds for them in a local exhibition or a small gallery if she could persuade them to take them.

How about the view from the studio, over the Downs?

She tried that as well and decided it was slightly more successful. She set up in her front garden and painted the views out over the small cliff. *Try a touch of burnt ochre for the shadows in the sea, just a touch mind, nothing too strong.*

She started to take her gear out, setting up in fields and on village greens. No help was available away from the cottage but when she brought her efforts home to finish off, there was always a little guidance that improved them.

One day she carried her gear down the rough path to the small beach below the house. It was a bit of a struggle and her foot slipped once or twice but she made it. She set up facing east and spent the afternoon there trying to capture the shoreline. No whispers. 'Perhaps he can't reach this far,' she thought.

Engrossed as she was in the beauty of the sunlit shore in front of her she didn't see the bad weather coming up from the west behind her. All at once the sun was covered and she realised she was cold. The sea was a lot rougher than it had been and she could see heavy rain coming. Scrabbling to save her work and her gear, as she started up the path the rain started to lash down. She slipped, turning her ankle painfully.

She could see that, whipped up by the wind, the incoming tide would cover the whole beach. She needed to get off the beach and up the cliff but found it very difficult being cold, carrying all her gear and with a foot that was extremely painful to walk on. She didn't want to leave anything behind. Her paints would be ruined, her easel would probably float away and she didn't want to leave one of the best paintings she thought she'd done.

Very faintly, *Don't worry, there's another way.*

It was so faint she wasn't sure she'd actually heard it. Was it her imagination running riot?

See that cleft in the rocks? It leads to a little cave. Go on. Try it.

It was certainly easier to cross the sand to the rocks than to try and climb the cliff. Yes, there was a cave. *Carry on going.* As she proceeded into the cave it rose in level

217

slightly but it was much easier to walk here on solid sea-worn rock than on the rough path up the cliff. Perhaps she could get above the sea level and wait out the tide and the storm. Or was she just trapping herself? Would the incoming tide fill the cave?

Keep going. I have a surprise for you.

After a few minutes, although she hadn't noticed the floor rising, she realised she was a lot higher than the level of the beach. *You could leave your stuff here and get it later. It'll be safe. But there's a way out.*

She carefully placed her paints and the new painting on a convenient ledge, keeping only her cloth shoulder bag and her easel to use as a makeshift walking stick. *Keep going.* She could hear the twinkle in his eye.

She rounded a large boulder and ahead of her she saw a set of steps. *Go on.* She climbed them. *This was an old smugglers' route. I found it one summer. Great isn't it?*

They were quite shallow steps, no real problem for her even with her painful ankle. They gently wove through the rock, a passageway wide enough for at least one person.

She came to the top of the steps and was faced with an old wooden door. There was an enormous circular handle on one side. *Try it then.* Turning the handle and pushing the door she was astonished to find herself in the hallway of her cottage. The door was faced with part of the panelling. Even having cleaned it, she hadn't realised there was a door there.

"Useful," she murmured, thrilled.

Very. Feel along the side of the panel. There's a catch.

She found it. Then she experimented by closing the door and opening it with the catch. It slid open silently every time.

Life went on. Her ankle eased after a few days of rest and judiciously applied arnica. The bad weather had set in and she probably wouldn't have left the house anyway. She was quite happy to sit in the window seat and watch the wild wind batter the bay.

She had kept in intermittent contact with her friends by email – no phone calls, too immediate – but had offered no invitations. One or two dropped hints about a visit but she put them off. She was quite happy living in seclusion with her whispers. Comfortable.

One day, from her front garden she saw an armada of small craft approaching, all with colourful sails. A yacht race. *Quick.* She rushed inside for her camera and took as many shots as she could as they passed. Then she started sketching. Even after the yachts had long gone she stayed there inserting more and more detail, trying to fix the conditions in her memory. The day clouded over and she realised she was cold so she took everything inside and up to her studio.

Marvellous. This needs to be large. It will make a wonderful painting.

She printed out the photos and using them and her sketches started to paint on the largest canvas she possessed. *How about elongating that mast a little? It might look better with a mistiness, not too much definition.*

And it did. When she had made the last stroke she stood back and admired what she knew to be the best work she had ever done.

What shall we call it? The Race?

"Yes, I like that."

This deserves to be seen, my lovely.

Ellie was nervous of contacting a reputable gallery. *Nothing to be nervous about; they're going to love you.*

Nevertheless, Ellie couldn't bring herself to make that first contact.

If it's still there, try the Sinclair Gallery in South Kensington.

She searched for the gallery on the web. Yes, it was still there. It was run by Stuart Sinclair, son of the founder, Alistair. Eventually she emailed the gallery, attaching photographs of *The Race* and a couple of the other paintings that she was happiest with. As soon as she'd pressed send, she regretted it. It was like dropping a letter in the post box and not being able to get it back. But she'd done it now.

And so she waited.

After two weeks Ellie decided the Sinclair Gallery wasn't interested in her work. 'Rude not to reply at all though,' she thought to herself. *Don't worry. They'll be in touch.*

She settled down to some story-book illustrating – it was after all her bread and butter work – considering the style she would use for a picture book about small wild animals. The phone rang.

"Hello?"

"Yes, hello," said the disembodied voice. "Is that Ellie Johnson?"

"Yes, speaking."

"Good afternoon, Miss Johnson. Stuart Sinclair here. I'm ringing about your paintings."

"Oh yes?"

"I'm so sorry it's taken so long to reply. I've been out of the country for the past three weeks and your email was left for my attention. Someone should have least have acknowledged it but I'm afraid I only have a temp in at the moment; my usual assistant is taking some personal leave."

"Oh, that's OK," Ellie reassured him. "I'm sure you're not too interested anyway."

"On the contrary," said Stuart Sinclair, "I'm very

interested. I'd like to meet you. Do you have more like these? Could you email photos? And I'd like to see the originals of course. Could you come here to the gallery? Or would it be more convenient for me to visit you? Anytime."

Ellie was taken aback at Stuart Sinclair's enthusiasm. She took a few moments to consider things. *Tell him to come here.*

Stuart Sinclair arrived the next morning having been driven down by his chauffeur. He was an elderly gentleman, possibly in his eighties Ellie judged, dressed conservatively with a ready smile.

They shook hands at the door. "How do you do Mr Sinclair?"

"Stuart, please. I'm hoping we'll get to know each other very well." Ellie invited him in and asked about the chauffeur. "Edmund is fine outside waiting for me. He has his flask of tea and his binoculars. He loves to watch the sea."

Ellie had arranged all her new canvases around the sitting room. She ushered him in and left him to look, excusing herself to make coffee.

When she returned, Stuart Sinclair was studying *The Race*. "This is the best," he said, "although the others are very good too. I'd like to exhibit you, all of these. Do you have any more? Could you produce more for an exhibition in, say, six months' time?"

Ellie sat down heavily in one of the easy chairs. "Probably."

Stuart Sinclair laughed and seated himself in the other chair. "I seem to be rushing you rather. I'm sorry. Let's calm down a bit. Tell me all about yourself."

Ellie explained that she was a children's book illustrator and showed him one of her books. He was polite but obviously not too impressed. "Delightful," meaning she supposed 'good enough for what it was'. She even told him about Alex and moving to the cottage. She did not mention the cottage whispering to her.

"I'm very keen on these paintings. Have you shown them to anyone else?"

"No, no-one."

"The thing is... the style reminds of someone. Have you ever heard of Jack Stabb? Probably not. He's an artist from long ago but you may have come across his work."

"Yes, actually I have heard of him. Why do you ask?"

"Because your paintings remind me a little of his work. My father discovered him. Well, I say 'discovered'. Jack walked in off the street one day with a pile of canvases under his arm. This was quite soon after my father had set up the gallery. Dad liked them and needed something to display so he paid for them to be framed and exhibited them. Jack became an overnight sensation. But this was back in the thirties and forties."

Ellie was a little nervous. Could she be accused of forgery or plagiarism or some such? "Why do my paintings make you think of him?"

"I don't quite know. Not the actual content. Jack painted his time, before the war. I think it's something to do with the depth, the use of colour. It's only an impression and you must realise I grew up with Jack's paintings; I know them all quite well. I doubt if too many other people would see a likeness."

"Did you know him?"

"Yes, well I met him but I was just a boy and he died before I grew up. I went to his cottage a few times with my father." Stuart rose and made his way to the window. "In fact it was very like this place although that's a child's memory. I suppose any cottage on the coast would seem similar."

222

"When I viewed this place I was told that Jack Stabb had lived here," Ellie told him. "That's why I've heard of him. I looked him up, saw a few of his paintings online."

Stuart stared at her for a few moments. "Goodness. Do you think you're channelling his spirit?" But then he laughed. "It must just be the way the light behaves here. Makes you use a similar palette."

Awkwardness over. Ellie had admitted the connection and Stuart hadn't paid any attention to it. He seemed to be one of the few that might notice Jack Stabb's techniques and had thought it a coincidence. No need to worry, no need to try and explain.

"I have some old photographs here. Would you like to see them?"

He produced three small black and whites photos. One showed two men standing in front of the cottage. "That's Jack and my father. I can see it's this cottage now." Another showed Jack and a young boy of about five. "That's Jack and me." The third showed both men and the boy laughing at a secret joke. "We got the postman to take that one." Although the images were small and monochrome, Ellie could see a tall handsome man, though looking older than his 40-odd years.

"Would you mind if I scanned these, so I have a picture of him?"

"Be my guest. I'll take in the magnificent view from your window while I'm waiting."

The scanning took only a few minutes. Printing out the pictures could be done later. She returned the photos to Stuart with thanks.

"Well," Stuart said, "I ought to be going but I would like to formalise things a bit. What would you say to a month's exhibition in October? For as many paintings as you can produce with the proviso that I have the final say?"

Say yes.

"Yes."

"I think you'll be a great success," Stuart said as he left. "I'm usually right about these things."

It was lovely to see Stuart again. Of course, 75 years have changed him considerably but it's still Stuart. Same smile.

It was lovely to see pictures of you. I'll print them out, frame them and put them on the wall.

I haven't changed a bit. Well my girl, we've got lots of work to do. How wonderful.

About the author

Julie Swan's background is as an electronics engineer and mathematician. She has been enjoying writing short stories and articles, some of which have been published, for over ten years after joining a local class. She is now part of a local ladies writing group: Pink Ink. Julie has a husband and twin daughters and lives in a lovely spot between the New Forest and the sea.

Index of Authors

Other Publications by Bridge House

Extraordinary

by Dawn Knox

From the furthest reaches of the universe, to the inside of a
cardboard box, assorted characters play deadly games with
their victims while others play practical jokes on angels or
dirty tricks on aliens. Some have good intentions, others are
scoundrels and a few are truly evil – but all of them are
EXTRAORDINARY.

"A wonderful collection of amazing stories. An enjoyable
read." (*Amazon*)

Order from Amazon:

Paperback: ISBN 978-1-907335-51-8
eBook: ISBN 978-1-907335-52-5

Citizens of Nowhere

edited by Gill James

Is a global citizen really a citizen of nowhere? This collection
reacts to this question and explores some possible answers.
Each story gives us a definition of one global citizen and
shows how this individual contributes to the world.

This time we approached several writers who we knew cared
about these matters and who also write beautifully. Other
stories also just fell into our laps – they had been submitted to
other anthologies and seemed to suit this one.

Citizens of Nowhere
an anthology

Order from Amazon:

Paperback: ISBN 978-1-907335-53-2
eBook: ISBN 978-1-907335-54-9

Tales from the Upper Room

edited by Janice Gilbert, Debz Hobbs-Wyatt and Gini Scanlan

Poems and Short Stories by the Canvey Writers, St Nicholas Group, who meet in the upstairs room…

You will be wowed by the dark tales: a modern day Little Red Riding Hood – as you have never seen her before. You will wait for the Reaper to come and you'll encounter ghosts in different forms. You will laugh at how Mavis and cat, Cuddles, and a glass of Lambrusco manage to start World War III, and how a job search lands aging Mr Montegoo the perfect job. You will read about war, about hate, and about love. You will encounter the power of what-if moments, love that endures, lovers that got away and the effect of the choices we make in life.

Proceeds from the sale of this book will be donated to Havens Hospices

Order from Amazon:

Paperback: ISBN 978-1-907335-19-8

www.ingramcontent.com/pod-product-compliance
Lightning Source LLC
Chambersburg PA
CBHW072234170626
46813CB00003B/1219